MW01248429

Am I
Mad. . .

AMY MAIDEN

authorHOUSE®

AuthorHouse™ UK
1663 Liberty Drive
Bloomington, IN 47403 USA
www.authorhouse.co.uk
Phone: 0800 047 8203 (Domestic TFN)
*   +44 1908 723714 (International)*

Published by AuthorHouse 09/18/2019

ISBN: 978-1-7283-9378-0 (sc)
ISBN: 978-1-7283-9379-7 (hc)
ISBN: 978-1-7283-9377-3 (e)

Print information available on the last page.

Change...

*is one of the hardest
lessons in life*

AMATEUR WITCH

I hope, I say I hope, what I really mean to say is that I have hoped, prayed, Stamped my feet, shouted out to the universe, begged, pleaded, commanded, demanded and finally when all else had failed and all doors seemed like they were closed, I just dropped down on my knees like a baby who is learning to take the first steps and bam, straight down on to the floor and I cried, I hysterically cried.

I need change!

I cried this to the source, the creator, the main guy, God, anyone! 'Is anyone there? I want change', I pleaded.

'Who is there?'

'Is there anyone there?'

'Can anyone hear me?' I shouted out, 'because if you can, I would like change, I need something to change, I would welcome change, I would embrace change, I would accept change. I desperately want something to change'.

I cried this to the walls of my apartment, my plants and my wooden statue of hear no evil. Calling all spirit guides, Gods and Goddesses. Sobbing and snivelling in true style to the nothingness of my apartment whilst staring at the Moon. Tears streaming down my face with the fully accelerated throttle of self pity.

'I am really unhappy, can you not see that?' I wailed at my plants.

I am more than just unhappy; I am dejected, dysphoric and I feel spiritless. My life is shit. What is wrong with me?

My sad little life is shit! I carried on with my tears, feeling comforted in my own sad little state of shitness. I am unhappy with my choice in friends, my choice in men, the bitchy backstabber and the bullies. I wanted to do so much better with my life. How did I end up here?

I am miserable, I grumbled.

I want this constant feeling of utter misery that has consumed my heart to disappear, the sadness to dissolve from my soul. I am sick of this small little town, with its small minded people.

Something has just got to change. Change is for the good, change is for the better and I want change right now I demanded. I hate my life!

As I was not really expecting anyone to listen to me, I got my ass off the floor, wiped my snotty nose with a tissue, slung myself on the sofa and began to compose myself.

'Why can't my life change?' I sighed.

Immediate transformation, I could just click my fingers and change my world. Just like that!

I could be zoomed up, recalled, reprogrammed and start afresh. I could have a transfer in life. I could go and play for another team, in another country, because this life I have got right now is shit. I feel shit.

I carried on continuously moaning, whining, complaining and grumbling to the walls of my apartment for the rest of the entire night. Taking great care that I pointed out exactly what was so shit about my life.

There is a saying- Mud sticks, let me tell you from my heart. How very true that particular saying is, when I say that it infectiously sticks to you like a bad smell. I can say this, I know, because I have been there. I've had the mud thrown my way. It is not nice, if truth be told it is rather shit, so I say open and honestly that this is true, very *very true*. Mud sticks.

Some years ago I had the chance to experience a real mud bath in Turkey. You climb in the therapeutic hot spring. The mud feels warm and milky against your skin. You then start to rub the mud over your body, smearing huge dollops on your arms and over your neck, how lovely it feels baking itself dry in the hot glorious sun. Casually you stroll over to the natural mineral of earths paddling pool, slowly and peacefully you immerse your body into the water and rinse away the mud, you are now feeling refreshed and revitalized with skin that is now silky and wonderfully smooth.

Then there is the human mud bath, which consists of the bitchy horrible people. The men, the woman, the straights, the gays and the drag queens who like to target others. These groups of people all form their little clans with their want to be leaders. If you don't conform to the beliefs and the ideas of this petty crew you are out of the crowd, End of. Poisoned darts are now to be thrown into your back for now and ever more.

There is also a saying that great minds have wills, average minds have wishes and small minds like to discuss other people. The town I live in is full to the brim of these small minded people, with their prejudice opinions and their narrow minded pea size brains. They are consumed in their own sad, pathetic excuse called existence. Each caught up in their own bullshit world, who have zero else going on in their meaningless miserable life other than bullying other people and therefore like to take great pleasure in causing misery to others. This type of person loves nothing more than to target an individual then callously bitch behind the intended victims back, with their mouths full of gossip, spreading lies like the plague. This is true and how this mud bath stinks, like the stinking tip where you dump all your rotten rubbish, discarded and left to decay, the smell is putrid, vile. It stinks.

This human mud bath is a very different kettle of fish, a totally different story altogether. It is nothing in comparison to the relaxing Turkish mud bath I enjoyed in the sun many years ago when life was once ace, before I felt the pain of betrayal, broken hearts, death and the slaughter of my reputation. This mud bath destroys the life of the victim, the target. There is definitely no strolling going on in this shit, you race to rinse the mud off, you are utterly surprised, gobsmacked even, at the amount of mud that has dried. It has dried hard, forming into thick crusty layers.

It takes quite a bit of dunking your body up and down in the clean water, but the water never seems to run clear. Frantically you start rubbing your body, desperately scrubbing at your skin trying to remove the mud, the putrid stinky mud. The mud is now stuck!

When you have had human mud chucked in your direction, you know it, you can feel it and you can sense it. You can smell it in the air, like the sweat pouring from the deceiver who has just committed the crime.

You two faced backstabbing bastard I would think to myself about the person who has slung the mud at me, but I put on a front, a brave face and I pretend that I do not care, that my feelings have not been hurt and I try to let it go.

But underneath the surface I am aware of the resentment that is starting to build up. I am left feeling choked, suffocated; I can feel my chest start to tighten, I am completely dumbfounded, mortified with that person, the mud throwing shit slinger, the adult bully.

Over and over again I run to the clean water, only to find the layers are rebuilding, as soon as I think that I have washed away the very last layer of the mud, I realize that I am being covered in yet more mud, only it has returned thicker and viler than before.

A person knows when they have had mud slung at them, the big catapult of shit that hits you full force in the face, the rumors, the whispers and the dirty snide glances.

I was not going to stand back whilst some cocky idiot slings a load of mud at me and tries to ruin my life, my reputation.

I went from being a confident, happy social butterfly, to wild rages, snot tears and tantrums. Anger, resentment, bitterness and pain - To experience the feeling of remorse the next morning, feelings of regret of Oh My! What have I done?!

'Why couldn't I just let it go?

'Why did I have to say something?'

I shout at myself that he or she was just not worth it. But I know why I just couldn't let things go, I know why I had to say something. My outbursts never made the slightest bit of difference to helping my situation. I only ever managed to make things a hell of a lot worse.

As I was sat down in my shit life thinking about the change I wanted, praying to a god I did not really know existed. Is he real? Is he there?

Is he a he?

Is he a she?

Is he a he/she?

Does he live in another place somewhere else above us? Does he watch down on us like we are little people in dolls houses, that he can just pick us up and play with us whenever he felt like it?

Is there a God?

I would ask myself over and over, if there is a God which religion does he belong to? I am not sure which religion I should join there are loads.

I moaned away to myself in my head, to have faith surly I must need a religion?

But you are not religious, the little voice in my head told me. You have never been christened, you never go to church -

4

But then who do I pray to?

I started to read as much as I could about different religions. I needed someone to pray to. Up until now all my heartfelt pleas for change have just been directed at anyone…the Sun, the Moon, the Creator, the source, the main man, God, Goddess, Angels and spirit guides but mainly my plants… I need someone to pray to.

Do I just say a prayer silently in my head?

Will God hear me? I thought about this for a bit; who do I choose? I was starting to get confused with the whole religion thing, but I was determined a religious path was the right path for me. I kept up with my search. I am on my way to being on my new path, my new religious path I declared to myself. The thing was, as I was coming across each religion I would think to myself, yes, I like that bit about it, but then again I am not really too keen on other aspects regarding that certain type of religion, it is not convincing me to sign up.

Or I would sway into another religion and think to myself … yes…I have cracked it. This certain religion has got some good things going on to suit me. Some parts of it I like but after spending a bit more time reading other people views, I would change my mind again. Leaving me then questioning my choice. I was just not sure.

I was not sold on the whole concept of the no sex before marriage malarkey.

I would frequently change my mind, almost daily to what religion I was now considering committing myself to. Or if a religious path was the right road for me. There are a lot of contradictions in convectional religion. I was confused, I could not decide.

'To be religious, I must need a religion right?'

'So which religion do you want to be' the little voice in my head asked.

I googled everything I could find on the internet about the different kinds of religions. I read articles, bits of the Bible and the Qur'an. I went to charity shops and purchased books on different cultures with different points of view. Why does everyone fight over which God is the one, the main man, the top dog? I would ask my plants.

'Because each one thinks that their God is superior' my little voice said.

Yes but which one should I choose?

I did not want to conform or reform at my age, I am already a mother

Amy Maiden

of two and have never been married. I knew I didn't want anymore children. 'My children are both young adults and family life didn't work out for me' I announced to my plants. I do not like being controlled by a man. I do not want to be tied down. I want to be free and already I was now living my life exactly the way most religions were against. Here I was living my life that most of the religions say that a woman is not supposed to do.

Why is that? I wondered.

I carried on reading, I soon discovered that there were quite a lot of different religions to choose from; Christianity, Islam, Hinduism, Chinese traditional religion, Buddhism, Primal- Indigenous, African traditional, Sikhism, Juche, Spiritualism, Judaism, Bahia, Jainism, Shinto, Cao Dai, Zoroastrianism, Tenrikyo, Unitarian, Rastafarianism, Scientology –

Not for me I moaned.

No definitely not, far too many rules in conventional religions and I have already broken far too many rules and according to the information I have read, if I choose a religion that most people follow I am already living in sin. I don't want to choose a religion that automatically makes my life a sin. I want something that I can have faith in and also be the woman I desire to be.

Can I not have a religion where a woman is free to make her own choices, to have sex when it suits her, with consent, whenever she pleases and live life without so called sin? I would ask, although I wasn't quite sure who I was asking.

I decided that I wanted a religion. My very own religion, I wanted a religion that suits me, suits my needs, a religious pick and mix. So I can be happy. I want my God and I'm not sure I ever want to get married, although I do not want to be a sexless spinster. I do not want to be a spinster, but if it turns out I might be I certainly don't want to be a sexless one I moaned on. I want to love again.

So in the search for my religion and who is God, looking at the many various religions I came across paganism... hang on I thought, this seems cool. Yes this is more like it, freedom for me, freedom for woman, it has nothing against marriage free sex. The woman in this religion, are valued for the beautiful creatures that we are. As without woman man would not exist. Yes this is it. This sounds more like me, definitely, a pagan I started to be.

I have got religion, I have got a faith, I shouted out to the world.

I am a pagan, Yes a pagan woman is me...

My birthday is also on the twenty fifth of December. Christmas Day - Is Christ real? Is it the son or the Sun? I asked my plants. As I imagined excitedly celebrating Pagan festivals. I could now add the traditional Christmas day with Yule/ winter solace on the twenty first of December, so I get a bonus, two celebrations at Christmas. A birthday party for me on Christmas Day after the magic of the winter solace.

In my head I was thinking I would no longer have to share my birthday with others. This thought enlightened me as I daydreamed. My birthday could become my day, a day for just me, but then I realized how much I love Christmas Day and giving and receiving presents.

This is it I have found my path. Christmas is an old Pagan tradition so it suited me fine. I love Christmas, I love Christmas Day.

The birth of Christ.

Is Jesus the son of God? Or is he the son of Christianity? Is Jesus real? I wonder who my God is.

I carried on with my thoughts happily chatting away to my plants. I do not want to be stuck in some loveless marriage with boring sex or worst still no sex at all. I can leave if things do not work out, we wouldn't even have to get married and even better we wouldn't have to live together if we choose not to. We could make our own choices and not be judge. We could just love each other for as long as it lasts and well if things between us do not work out then that is fine. I will just meet someone new and start over again. Yes I like this religion, it is all about love.

Being a pagan is relatively easy. You support and worship Mother Nature and you recycle. Pagans pursue their own vision of the Divine as a direct and personal experience. Paganism is the ancestral religion of the whole of humanity.

Modern Pagans are not tied down either by the customs of an established religion or by the dogmas of a revealed one, are often creative, playful and individualistic, affirming the importance of the individual psyche. There is a respect for all of life and usually a desire to participate with, rather than to dominate other beings. It is all about love.

I am sold, committed, yes I am a Pagan I announced.

So I was settling into my religion or that is what I thought, when one evening I got side tracked whilst I was googling, this night I came across

Witch Craft. As I read more on witches and the craft I started to wonder, could I be a witch?

I found I was being intrigued, more than intrigued if truth be told, I was becoming boarder line obsessed, with spells and witchcraft sites.

I would spend hours reading about other witches and the happy life they had, HARM NONE was the message everyone would say. This religion sounded good. All the people are also into Mother Nature, they are also animal loving and caring. This is it I thought to myself, bang on, this is the right religion for me. I have found my true path. I integrated being a Pagan with becoming a Witch.

My childhood vision of witches flying around on broomsticks with pointy noses, black teeth, cursing evil through the night was after all something we fear as kids. No witches rock! That was it. I am a Pagan-witch. So now all those thoughts were replaced with images of nice witches doing well for our planet, saving the rain forest and celebrate eight seasonal festivals called Sabbaths, Craft rituals, like all Pagan rites, are often conducted out of doors and I love being outside I thought to myself, and involve simple rites to celebrate the seasons and the gift of life. Craft ritual is a means of contacting the Divine beyond our individual lives, but also a way of understanding our inner psyche and contacting the Divine within.

Witchcraft is a path of magic and love, the movement of a deep poetry of the soul, a sharing and joining with the mysteries of Nature and the Old Gods.

I read lots of information about my new faith, but I did not know any witches in real life, no one had a sign attached to their house and there were no church as such that you could just walk into and declare 'hi my name is Maggie I would like to become a witch? and you certainly cannot go up to random folk and say 'hi, I am trying to find a religion I don't suppose you are a witch are you, as I am searching for my path, I am looking for a religion and I quite fancy the idea of becoming a witch?'

I found people to be incredible private when it came to talking about their religion. Do not talk about religion or politics was the message heard loud and clear. Or people would not dare to mention they are of Pagan religion to a non religious person such as me. Are people still really worried about how Christianity burnt the witches for not conforming to their rules? I wondered.

I really fancied the idea of becoming a witch. I said to my plants. I am a witch already…

And I have always loved candles, there is something hypnotic about the flame. I soon bought lots of candles, different colors, different sizes and I would drive to the country to pick wild flowers or send my son in a garden to steal a flower, when my son was younger of course. My son and I back in the day went along to Tia Chi every Tuesday evening for a few months, just on the outskirts of our town and we would drive past big beautiful gardens and it was only ever one flower from one garden that I got him to take. We had some fun flower picking it was good funny times, times you cannot buy. By now my son was older enough to be board of pebble or shell collecting. Flower stealing gave him a puffed out glow on his chubby cheeky boy-man face, I would send him on his mission and wait a few houses away with my engine running, he would jump out of the car like lightening, pick me a flower, hoping he would not get caught and get shouted at by the garden owner. Then once he had grabbed the flower he would leg it back to the car laughing his head off. The garden owner on their way to confront. Smiling, my son then handed me the flower. Unforgettable moments. Happy memories.

I used the flowers to cast my spells…flowers picked with love.

I would also buy fresh flowers, flowers are lovely around the home. I would try writing my own poetry and then casting my own little spells, HARM NONE and FREE WILL being of the up most importance.

I was now casting my little spells here there and everywhere. Each spell I was sending with love, the love vibe to the universe. I was not taking magic to seriously as I am not a witch right!

I want my own house, so I wrote a spell for a house.

- Spell for my house. -

I wrote this in big letters across the top of a sheet of paper

I would like a house to have a back garden, where the sun shines in all day. I would like to see the moon from my bedroom window.

I would like nice neighbours.

I would like my home to have gas central heating, which has also a combination boiler.

I would like a bathroom with a shower over the bath and a toilet in the bathroom.

I would like double glazing,

I would like my home to have a living room and a kitchen big enough for a dining table, washing machines, a fridge freezer, a dish washer and a tumble dryer.

My house will have two bedrooms that will fit in a double bed in each one.

I would want my house to be happy and loving.

I want my house to be energy efficient.

I want to be able to park my car outside my home.

I finished my spell, and recited it to the top of my head and then I waited for the full moon. On the night of the full moon, I lit my candles and I sang out the song of my spell, whilst I burnt the paper and then scattered the ashes in the breeze.

I sat for ages thinking, wondering where I am going next, buzzing around momentarily happy in my little world, in my daily routine, like the bee that has got all the pollen he needed from the beautiful flower. I was living in happy land. This was the my religion. a religious path for me.

Up and down on the train journey of life!

So when did my life start to breakdown, on what day? How did I end up here?

On the surface everything was honky dories, I worked as a hair stylist. I lived in a luxury apartment, I was earning a decent wage so why was I complaining? Inside, I felt something strange start to happen. I started to be miserable. I am sick of my life, I would constantly moan to the universe. Its shit, it sucks. I go to work every day and for what? I protested. life is shit.

I am fed up with making everyone look nice, I have no free time, all I do is work, work, work and work, early mornings, late nights. I want a summer off I told mid air and I want a house. I was getting tired with the bullshit.

I soon started casting more and more spells.

Rid me of negativity.

From people who's intent is to harm.

Erase them from my life.

Wither consciously or subconsciously.

Erase them from my life.

If the hurt is malicious, let them receive the hurt back.

And times it by three. I wasn't really sure why I times it by three, but I read that what a witch does, so I did as a witch would do.

No longer do I want any negativity from either myself or others affecting my life.

My aim is to love – to accept all my sisters and brothers.

To live in harmony.

Bring friends closer and send enemies away.

Allow me to get the best for myself for what is the rest of my time on earth.

My life train was up and down…

The more moaning and whining I did, the whinier and moanier I became.

Life was shit, it sucked and it had also become unfair.

I was drawing in negative energies, negative vibes, joining the crew of the underworld. I was not grateful for all the good in my life I was finding flaws with everything. I had a total lack of understanding, as I whined and bitched at the unfairness of things, the injustice, how shit life was to the universe, things started to go wrong.

So my life was becoming shitter and shitter. What was happening to me? Was something changing?

I whined constantly. Whinge. Whinge. Whine. Whining my days away.

I would go about my day casting little spells, making little wishes or saying a prayer. I did not know which was which, casting spells seemed romantic reciting poetry, relaxing in a hot bubble bath using different oils, different coloured candles. Driving out somewhere in nature and sitting under the moon or chilling by the ocean under the Sun, who wouldn't want to be a witch. Casting magic by the power of the Sun. the Earth and the Moon, I command thee….

Was I being unrealistic with my spell casting? I had no savings for a deposit to buy a house or to have a summer off.

I had practically forgotten all about my early days of spell casting as I started sinking deeper in to the shitness, the great big shit hole that was slowly becoming my life.

Everything started to go wrong as soon as I did something it back fired and down further I would spiral. I was experimenting with magic but it was not real right, it was only for fun. Yet inside my head I started to believe in the power of the universe, the power of thought. As my days became shitter and shitter, my thoughts became darker, soon my thoughts were dangerously borderline, some people would even say slightly twisted but being an amateur witch I did not care. I would avoid making any horrible spells as I would call them, curses or hexes, No Way! My spells to me were still the same but without me realizing my intention had changed. My spell casting was not coming from a place of love and peace for mankind my intentions were becoming negative.

I would bitch to the universe that everyone else in the world had a great life, a job they loved doing, happy relationships and all I get is shit people who bully or those who after I go out of my way for them, showed them kindness, shown loyalty, they stab me in the back.

I started to think how people had mistreated me. I never said anything to anyone at the time because I did not want to upset anyone.

I avoided confrontation…until despair kicked in.

'You don't want to upset people' the voice pronounced..

'Why would you give fuck if you upset people who have treated you badly?' Tell them all to fuck off, accept it and let it go' the voice carried on.

Things that I wanted to say to people for ages, people that had hurt me, started to come into my thoughts.

'Tell them what you think then end the relationship' the voice said sternly.

And that is how it began.

Everyone who had every mistreated me, cheated, lied or falsely accused got it.

Well I have been injustice and I have had enough of people using me and treating me like crap, always laying the blame on me.

My private life was gradually starting to slip into the darkness – casting spells, spending my time collecting different materials, buying the correct size and colour of the candle, knowing the different moon phases. I spent my spare time writing poetry for my spell. I had become a casting spell addict. Tooled up with my wooden mini caldron. Yes a witch I am!

So my life was now shit and the more I started to realize people had treated me like shit, the shitter I felt. I would think back and think how dare you, do you think you're going to get away with that. The harm none principle was being stretched a little each and every day. I had no idea about protection.

Protection from what? I would say. Who do I need protecting from?

My own little ritual of protection was fun, I imagined I was wrapped up in a big silver bubble, surly that was enough?

Was it not? I thought that was all it took.

And I was getting impatient with some of my spells and was starting to wonder if magic really did work. But it must work I have chosen this religion, this religion is for me. I chose it right, I would tell myself. don't loose faith.

Feeling the great big injustice that was my life. I started to wonder who my friends are. Certainly not the one who had slept with my boyfriend or the one from my past, that not only wanted to take my best friend away from me, she also wanted to be me, have my life. I could see jealousy on her face the day her boyfriend said I had lovely feet.

'What about my feet' she snarled at him

'Yours are massive for a woman' he said innocently.

'Well she has got my life now, I hope her life is as great as can be' I said sarcastically to my plant.

I am so sick of this life, the judgments, I complained. The jealous women whose men I have refused, the two faced bastards. The fake younger woman who is in a relationships with a rich older man for the status and the cash. She who looks down on me, bitches behind my back. Everywhere I look I can see the crapness. Or the new boyfriend that puts me down to his pals in the hope that none of them will like me, making it virtual impossible for me to get it on with any of these men behind his back… like I would want to.. everybody hates you he would tell me… I became paranoid.

Yes my life is shit!

Total shitness and not giving a shit and with shitness and shit the darker my days became.

I refused to do what I would call any harmful spell until it happened. Another poisoned dart flung at me full force that landed straight into my heart. That is it you fucking bastard. I paced around the room trying to justify to myself that this was OK to do. A passing fling that had ended when death arrived, he had started to gossip and throw darts, he told everyone that I am a lunatic, that after our argument I smashed his furniture!

'I am not a lunatic' I told my plants.

'I went back to his the morning after our argument and nothing was smashed. He wasn't in. He has already left for work, I left and posted the key behind me. Can people just go round saying shit like that to people about other people?' I shouted, marching around the living room, steam blowing out of my ears. 'The fucking dirty low down piece of crap that he is' I ranted- 'well that is it'.

I imagined him in my head, then I said I hope he gets stomach ache…

Give him cramps in the night, I hope he shits his pants when he is playing pool…

By the power of the Sun, Earth and the Moon…

He deserves this you know I would then explain to the universe, what he did was a shit thing and I am not having it anymore. No more backstabbing, no more bullying. No more lies. I want all fair weathered friend out of my life, I don't want any false people even if I end up with no people, no friends I don't care – so I was living my shit life, when shitness became the norm.

I was now seeing people drop out my life at random speed, some I was bemused and didn't give a stuff but others I got really angry and upset with, people I had considered friends, close friends. People were now doing bizarre stuff, random fucked up actions, they were turning, oh and how I was learning.

I was casting spells to remove false friends but it hurt when I discovered I had false friends, friends I had considered to be my close friends.

I was careful in my wording harm ye none, but added - like for like - we reap what we sow - give back what they give to me, I started to take witch craft very seriously. I also started learning how to remove bad intentions and send the spell with love again. I did not want to harm anyone, well only the bullies and the backstabbers I told the universe. I am just fed up with people throwing mud my way. I am sick of the shit. After a short period of time I was pretty much spelled out. I had cast a spell for everything, only then did I start to learn about how important protection is and the law on the craft.

I wrote my first protection spell. I read it over and over again until I could recite it. I sang my spell every day for the next few months;

By Divine light, the Sun and the Moon, wrap me in a spear of light, keep me protected from harm day and night, guide me towards the gates of eternal life. lead me to infinity. Mother Nature, the land and the sea, wrap me in love and carry me…

I started reading everything I could about protection – from what though?..

I was a total beginner but I already considered myself to be some sort of high priestess, a Goddess, right up there with the top dudes. But without years of studying that it takes I was being somewhat deluded. Any woman who buys a candle calls themselves a witch my friend used to tease.

But being in my world, being safely protected in my bubble I was more than safe or so I thought.

Patience has never been my virtue, hurry up I can't wait, will it ever happen… so instead of letting things be, I started meddling deeper into witchcraft. I purchased tarot card and began studying each one until I knew every tarot card there was. I started contacting the spirits for guidance and support, calling to the spirit of life. I was meddling in magic, thinking everything in my world, well it was going to be bloody marvellous. I chanted the words to my spell for protection everyday in preparation for my final spell, totally unaware and unprepared that I was already putting my spells out to the universe – the power of thought. Law of attraction. Magic and Prayers.

Not long after people had started dropping out of my life like flies, they were now accusing me of stealing or some other made up nonsense. How dare they I thought. I am no thief. People gossiping, my ears were on fire with all the lies and deceit. I was getting extremely pissed off with the poisoned darts that kept penetrating into my back. I would sit and meditate, visualizing pulling each of the darts out of my back, nine darts, then throwing them straight back to the rightful owner –

Return to sender address unknown, by the power of the Sun, the Earth and the moon.

And of course I would times it by three,

This was my new way of thinking; trouble was I had become a target for blame. people's true nasty colors were now shining through. Who could I trust?

As I began to delve deeper and deeper I also got really involved in meditation and the whole astral projection, out of body experience, lucid dreams started to happen and nightmares began.

I was struggling with the whole concept of trying to think about nothing as my mind was always racing.

It is really hard to think about nothing.

My mind constantly filled with shit, muddled thoughts of mixed emotions, death, heartbreak. What has happened to me?

Who am I?

What has happened over the years?

I am not who I want to be!

I would ask my plants, I gave them names…spider, yuk and giz, who by now I loved and cared for, watered and nurtured. I very rarely ventured out - unless I was working - if I did not have to, I would stay in and talk to the Sun or the Moon or to my plants. I was spraying fresh water on their leaves and wiping away the dust, praying for change.

Well that's someone else gone and a little bit further down I would sink.

I was in total denial. My life was slipping into the danger zone but I carried on like I was wearing a cloak and a tiara. I can rule the world! Yes of course you can the little voice would say. I am not sure where I read this saying, but I adopted it as if it was my own.

My life had become so far away from my dreams, my desires. What was my master plan to be!

I was turning my life into a fantasy. I did not want this life full of jealousy, mistrust and judgement. I wanted change. I needed change.

I was being pulled back and forth, back and forth, going round and round the merry go round of life in the shit.

As I sat there one morning, looking out of the window. I asked…'Did he, the piece of crap who tried to ruin my social reputation, passing fling, get stomach ache?'

And if he did, how painful do you think it was?

Not long after I had been thinking those thoughts, I started to clean my living room. I walked into the kitchen got a clean cloth, came back in the living room and went over to wipe the table, for some strange reason instead of wiping it, I knelt down and blew the bits of pencil sharpenings that littered the table.

Something went into my eye, something sharp. It felt like a little sharp piece of wood, a sharpening that was now slicing into my eye ball, tears instantly started streaming down my face.

Fucking hell, I don't believe it I screamed. My eye instantly puffed up, how did that happen? What happened?

What the fuck!

My eye started to swell at a rapid pace. I grabbed a trilby hat from the cloakroom to cover my eye and walked as fast as I could to the chemist, each foot step causing more excruciating pain, the sharpening was repeatedly stabbing against my eye ball.

The pharmacist looked at my eye "you would be better off going to the hospital" she said very kindly, shaking her head side to side as she held my face in her hand to inspect my eye, 'it will probably cause an infection'.

'I cannot go to the hospital' I told her and I bought an eye lotion with a little eye bath and I went straight home. Filled the mini bath with the solution and sat for the next few hours with the solution on my eye. Praying over and over, hoping that my eye would be OK. Please don't let me go blind I begged.

So once more my day had become shit. I had to cancel work and with no work - no money. I hated canceling work. I very rarely, if ever rang in sick.

As the afternoon approached, I was sat with the eye bath on trying to sooth my eye. Repeatedly topping the mini eye bath up with fresh liquid, thinking how the fuck did that just happen.

I cannot believe that has just happen!

What are the chances of that happening?

Then I remembered my question of the morning. No way! It couldn't be I thought. No... No way. Was this the kind of pain I had been inflicting?

'Take it off him' I demanded, 'take it off me, actually just take it off him, this is painful, I do not hate him, I don't even dislike him that much to cause this sort of pain'.

'Take it off him, I deserve it, I created it, whatever he did it was only words, stick and stones may break my bones words will never hurt me. This is horrible, he did not hurt me enough for him to go through this everyday'

'OK, so he turned into a nasty piece of work, slating me, slagging me down, telling lies, but this, I wailed at the universe, 'you deal with punishment. I am sorry' I desperately pleaded, totally convinced my sore eye was showing me the exact amount of pain I had been inflicting on another using witchcraft.

'Take it off him now' I begged.

After a few hours the tiny piece of sharpening came out of my eye and my eye started to go down, the swelling was starting to reduce, then my sore eye healed. I was left with ruby red whites of my eyes for the next few days.

Over the next few days I started to think about the spells I had cast. Shit, I did not want to think what the results of all these spells would be. Was I to try and stop them before they reached the target?

I didn't even know who the targets were. I had just sent the daggers from in my back, the poisoned darts back to the sender.

For the first time I was thinking about consequences of my actions, my spells, and started to think what the fuck!

Now what have I done. I started telling myself off.

Why have I been meddling in something I know absolute nothing about? I am not trained, I have not studied.

You are not yet good enough to go round casting spells. You love cooking but you wouldn't enter the master chef competition, so why for fucks sake are you practising witch craft! Voice said.

Because you have purchased a few candles, read the few basic principles, you have not only decided that you are now a witch, you have become a high priestess, a Goddess, Witch craft is a religion. A religion about love.

So I ask the questions -

Is magic real? Am I a witch?

I start to ask myself - Who am I?

What do I want from life?

SNOT, TEARS AND TANTRUMS

The morning after the rage the night before, I am woken to the initial blankness and then the horrible dread that starts to kick in. So who is it that I am unable to look in the face today? Who did I rant at?

Total memory blank, I know the feeling it has now become less frequent almost virtually rare, hearing the words 'you was in a state last night' and of course I feel ashamed - What is wrong with me? I am now on the ship of self loathing and of course no one gives a dam, no one cares and nobody is willing to give away any free love, not today, not on this ship anyway, no not a chance, no one is being kindhearted, not by any means. The overwhelming feeling of sickness in the pit of my stomach, 'I haven't been let off the hook' I moan into thin air. The headache, the pounding headache that feels as if one has been coshed with a hammer that penetrates into my skull with the slightest movement. The flash backs, fucking hell the flash backs come flooding in. I don't want to remember but dear God do I want to know.

This is of one of those feelings I cannot fully describe; puffy bloodshot and dilated eyes, no vivid memory, not yet anyway, just bits and pieces...best bits for later...The little voice would say.

Pictures are playing in my mind to the drum beat of the overwhelming sickness that medicine is unable to cure.

I found out that people can be incredible liars, downright dirty rats. Yet another two faced back stabbing wanker I would think. By now I had started to distrust. I had stopped seeing the good in people once I had sniffed out the bad in them, so I started to play little games with them, to test them. Test my own intuition see who my real friends are. I was sick of the bullshit and the pretence.

At first this was just fun but when I get someone screaming I spilt drink on her laptop causing a top scale performance. Now that is just fucked up.

I tried to explain it was just a drop, that there was nothing wrong with the laptop, but I am only making things worse trying to apologize to the over dramatic drama queen, her not being too eager to let it drop, she was screaming I was asked to leave.

We all think that we know the people around us. It is not about how many people you know or how many people you might meet for lunch or maybe have a few beers in your local pub with, or who you chat to in town. How many of us know who are real friends are?

I mean real friends.

I had my very own in built bullshit detector and it was beeping to the max!

I was fed up with all the bullshit, the bullshit that had become my life. The nasty camps, the woman with their fake hair, fake tan, fake nails, fake eyelashes and their fake, false personalities. The men with their spray on tans, tight tee shirts and muscles made from steroids, who swan around like they are something special. I had now become associated with petty people and now they were covering me in the putrid mud.

I had worked my ass off to build my clientele, to build my reputation, to become a stylist… For what!

I would hear things about me and think I didn't do that, I never said that, but that was how my life became. I was the target. My name is stuck in the mud and life becomes shit. I stopped telling my side. I gave up. It did not matter anyway, not anymore, no one would believe me.

Waking up the next day knowing what had happened. I mean really knowing what had happened is a great accomplishment. I look at them and think…

You'll be sorry you did that.

I would almost try and telepathically infuse this in their brain. Is it because people think I will not remember.

So now I have no choice but to execute the person from my life. But the thing is I let things build up instead of dealing with shit when it arrives, as I do not want to cause a fuss. Is it OK when a large woman grabs me by the throat because she had been on a three day alcoholic binge bender and I fail to turn up to do her daughter's hair the next day. I am now the let down. Or when I had been punched in the face and the nasty piece of work tries to tell me that I fell down the stairs, then tells people I attacked her. I fail to go to work and again, I am the let down. It is me who is letting another person down. Do people think that because of a few psychotic blackouts I have them all the time? Or is it that mud sticks! Why didn't I say what had happened? Because I always try to keep the peace and not get other people involved.

It then starts to fester inside. Tell the fucking truth!

Why should I care if people think I have let them down? The thing is I do care. I am not made of stone and I cannot let it go. It bubbles inside my head, like a kettle full of cold water slowly getting hotter and hotter, until it finally boils. Then all the hurt emotions that I have tried to ignore, that I have tried to bury, rise to the surface and I am then left thinking hang on a minute what you have done to me is diabolical, vulgar, disgusting. How could you? Then boom...Emotional overload!

When people are used to you acting in a way even you know you can. It is easy for someone to switch the blame, running around with their bullshit getting their side of the story in first. Is it not the case that those who strike first admit their ideas have given out!

It was not just a drop of wine that I had spilt on the drama queen's laptop her screaming like a bitch at me. It was now a whole glass, I wouldn't be surprised if it she was insisting that I split the whole bottle leaving the laptop now fucked and totally ruined... Big dramas.

No amount of apologizing would calm down this oscar winning performance the drama queen had going on, everyone rushing to her attention, so as a nice peace offering, I offer to collect her laptop the next day and take the machine for repair. I then leave.

So what does a person do?

I get up the next morning and I drive back to where the drama happened to collect the laptop, even though I knew there was nothing wrong with electrical device. I take the 'broken' devise to my friends house. I turned it on and call big drama asking her for the password so we could log on.

Such a big fuss!

I enter the Password feeling that after all the shit it has caused me, how yet again I am made to look like a prat, that I am entitled to a little nosey - A little snoop inside Madame's laptop. What a load of shit! I thought we were friends.

It can quite plainly be a right eye opener, not only for the shit slingers but also for me the target, when I know and they know I know the truth, of course being the perfect target for someone who is experiencing a little jealously or bitchiness, who would like nothing more than to make me look a fool and get rid of me from the crew.

The miss look at me the one who thinks I am so much better than you, look at you your shit. I have got everything. Then why are you jealous of me?

I am not better than you I am no worse than you, you are my equal.

I was devastated with some of my so called friends and my work mates. They all knew what was happening, the bitchiness that was going down, the set up that was about to take place, they had all joined in, all took their side on the winning team and also engaged in this human mud bath of catapulting shit. I have learnt to accept this. Sometimes good things have to fall apart so better things can take their place.

Is that what they say? I hope so.

After a period of time the constant piles of shit that kept repeatedly hitting me was now sticking and it was starting to get heavy, to weigh me down. It had by now began to have an effect on my life, the shit was now grinding me deeper down into the shitness. I was falling in the pit.

I never got quite enough satisfaction that I knew the real story.. So I already know it, so what.

I wanted the truth.

'You cannot force people to tell the truth' little voice would say. 'Why can I not make people tell the truth?'

Power of truth...

I know the truth and they know it, so I started to figure that just the very knowing that I know makes them out to be more of a fool. So who's the fool?

I have seen many people act this way over the years, bitching, back stabbing. The beauty industry is a bitchy place and working as a stylist listening to others bitch and moan about each other in the staff room is painful and at first it used to upset me, really upset me like I was experiencing deja vu, it's like shafting the wheat from the corn. As they think they are above the target and then they turned on me. I became the target.

I would get blamed for everything or set up for something, my equipment would go missing at work, or the tint I asked one of the juniors to mix was wrong. With so much pressure I was under at work I should have never mixed business with pleasure. The missile was to be fired at me the target for disaster, for they knew after, in the morning I wouldn't remember a thing. But to see how shocked and ashamed they were when it turns out I did not out have a blackout and how proud I was of myself for sticking to my plan of staying in control. Knowing I could remember - I can see it in their eyes, the window of the soul. That they are telling lies.

The dirty little snakes.

I just get these vibes when a person is telling lies, a feeling that I know.

I get a strange sensation when I know something is going to happen. I do not know how I know, I just know. I've ignored the signs far to many times and always regretted it. That little voice in my head that's warning me. Not really believing in the voice I hear. so I go against advise, throw caution to he wind and did things my way. Alcohol and emotions bad move.

My early phase of psychosis, saying my prayers, casting my spells, calling on the dead! Having psychotic attacks with the voices in my head! I was mixed up.

One evening I was hanging out with a group of friends, my friend's new girlfriend was high on drugs.

'Drugs working? I asked this woman, not thinking anything of it

'what are you talking about, I'm not on drugs' she yelled at me and started to get really upset.

Other friends started being slightly offish with me, unable to believe I would ask such a question. I couldn't quite believe the words had popped out of my mouth either, I meant no harm. Hey if she wants to take drugs... I always seem to say stuff when I should have kept it as a thought, Out my mouth the thought would pop before I realized what I was saying. I decided the best thing I could do was leave. After a few more weeks of my friend dating this woman, it turned out I was spot on, she had been on drugs, she was a drug addict. I was telling the truth.

How did i know? I have got no idea.

Slipping into the habit of self destruction now and then was relatively easy.

My life was so far away from how I wanted it to be, I wanted change. I really wanted something to change.

What I got was far from what I expected.

Life is like playing snakes and ladders. I climbed my way to the top then seeing the end in sight, I am hit with shit and I slide backward down the ladder. Concrete is now pouring over me by the tons, gallons and gallons surrounding my body. Causing my world to come crashing down around me. Life is a drag carrying all this weight, I am down in the dumps, life is totally shit. I scream - Change my life!

I climb back up again. Carry on with the game of life. Then I hear it, I hear the voice, a faint little voice...Err what do think you're doing? Get back down here lady!

What- Am I mad? Am I talking to myself?

Did I just talk to myself? The words came out of my mouth! And backwards I slide. I am sliding in to the concrete and I can't breathe, my world is falling apart. So I go on a bender, a booze binge, crying like a baby I want things to change. I black it out - I get it out my system, I then pick myself up, give my head a wobble, stand up straight and shout out loud, 'I wanted change to make things better, not to make things worse'. I am starting to think that I am- I am going mad! Then I realize I am screaming at my empty apartment.

I then start the process of picking myself up and getting ready to tackle the ladder once again.

So when things in my life are starting to turn shit as my life way fast becoming completely shit. I sat down and thought about my job.

My job is shit!

I thought about all the jobs I have had.

I had worked incredible hard to build my career and my reputation. My reputation was tested a number of years ago when I worked for a hair salon I will now call noxious. I wanted to move away from this salon. I wanted to try another salon, I wanted more money but noxious had different ideas. They weren't as keen on my plan as I was. This salon did not want to lose the income my clients brought in for their business. And I had a huge client base, I worked long hours to build a good clientele base.

I wanted to leave the salon but I also wanted to be able to tell my clients, inform them where I was going, where my new work place would be.

I had worked my backside off, I mean really long hours, the selfish bastards. My work mate who I classed as a friend had stitched me up, told my bosses that I had been offered a better job so they now knew I was about to jump ship. I didn't know my boss knew about my job offer.

They set me up, I became the target.

Why didn't they let me tell my clients? I asked my plants 'why didn't they allow me to give people the choice of staying in their salon, or moving to a new salon with me?

I was suspended on gross misconduct.

So in order to try and run from the start of the shit, which itself was becoming shit, shit life, shit job. Lies followed me around, I would get a new job in a new salon and my new boss would then receive an ominous phone call and the topic being of course me. It didn't matter that I took them to court or that all of their witness backed out in the end. Oh it's perfectly fine to tell people bullshit but they will not get up in front of a judge and swear it's truth.

No mud sticks and the more I tried to run from the shit the more bullshit they just kept on chucking.

Until finally I get offered and accepted a job, a senior stylist position, in the salon where I was originally going to work, before shit started to get chucked. I had bounced around the town jumping from salon to salon running from the shit and was finally at the place that was the reason the shit began. Here I was in the salon that I wanted to work in. I was happy and relieved. Thank fuck! My train journey of life was taking a mini breather.

It did not take long before the shit caught up with me. Nasty letters about me were now arriving at my new salon, to my new boss putting suspicion into people's minds, making me an easy target.

Things were all good for a few years, I worked hard rebuilt my client base but after a few years my boss then accused me of stealing. How mud can stick.

I would work late most nights and would lock up the salon. This one particular evening I had arranged to go on a dinner date with my son, I have always had one night a week when I took my kids out for a meal. I was running behind time, so I got his dad to drop our son off at the salon, my son waited for me whilst I finished my last clients hair. I then cut my sons hair. When I was finished I cleaned my area and then I went into the back and checked the back door was locked and removed the key. Now the bizarre thing was I put the key for the back door in a totally different place to where it is usually stashed. I do not know why I changed the hiding spot,

I just did. I then set the alarm, locked the main entrance door and went off for an evening with my child.

The next morning I arrived at work on time, which doesn't happen very often with me. My boss who also usually comes dashing in at the last minute was also on time, she was with the junior in the back area of the salon looking for the back door key.

'Where is the key Maggie?' My boss snapped at me.

'Oh it's here' I replied, going to fetch the key from where I had put it.

I still had no idea why I had put the key in a different place, I could not explain it. I then handed over the back door key to the junior so she could smoke her cigarette in the back yard. My boss stood next to my equipment cupboard and started getting out the client record cards for the day.

The junior I will now call Fatso was looking flustered, I paid no attention to her, I put my bag down and took off my coat, and noticed the Large GHD hair straighteners were not on the usually trolley.

'Where are the large GHD's?' I asked, as I thought I would sort my own hair out before my first client of the day arrived.

Big drama... The GHD's had gone missing.

'I haven't seen em' chipped in fatso

'Did you not use them before you left to straighten Toris hair?' I inquired.

After refreshing fatso's memory that she did in fact use the large GHD's, both of us, fatso and me, then started to search the salon. I searched the in the front of salon I couldn't find the GHD's so I went back into the back. My boss was still standing by my cupboard then my boss accused my son of stealing them.

'Your son was here, has he taken them?' my boss shouted.

I was mortified.

'If my son was going to steal a pair of GHD's which he would never steal, he would have taken the extra slim pair, so he could do his hair not the larger ones' I was now fuming. 'How dare you accuse my child of stealing' I seethed at my boss

Big mistake!

Suddenly realizing she had no choice fatso asks my boss to move out of the way and pulls the GHD's out of my cupboard where I keep all of my equipment, not shared salon equipment. A guilty look spread right across fatso's face.

Fucking hell she was better than a magician! I knew I hadn't put the GHD's in my cupboard.

It was a blessing I had swapped the stash place for the key or fatso would have had the GHD's out of that back door and set me up for theft before any other staff member had arrived for work.

Typical.

The next blow is my boss then had the audacity to accuse me of fiddling cash. I was livid. After each client I would write out a receipt, noting down the cash amount and the name of my client. We worked on a fifty - fifty basis so this let me know what I had made that day and would also let my boss know how much I had charged each client and what service I had provided and here she was in my face blaring her fat face off that I was stealing cash. Gobbing off right there for all to hear, even the clients who had already arrived for their appointment could hear her, she did not care in her wild rage because I am thick with mud, so it's perfectly OK for her to insult me in public. Call me a thief.

Who the fuck does she think she is screaming in my face.

So I thought to myself now this is proper shit. It was not worth her having a word with me in private oh no because mud sticks. My boss had gossiped with Fatso before even approaching me, because it has got to be true right.

What a complete arse she had looked, I mean a right twat, when I marched through the salon and showed her the appointment diary and the till receipts for the day of the mystery theft and I pointed out that she had got two receipts mixed up, as I had two women in the salon that day who were called Trisha. Two price receipts different cash amounts.

You stupid woman!

I did not steal.

How mud sticks!

I was not fiddling cash. I am certainly not a thief. She had got the completely wrong receipt. But to me our relationship from that very second was over. It just took me a week or so longer for me to register this information my mind.

Without pausing for breath, I moaned incessantly throughout the night on the subject of how shit my life was and how I was now sick of the shit and I had also become cured of running from the shit.

Quit then, the faint little voice sang in the back of my head.

Just quit? Quit just like that?

Yes quit.

OK I will. I then sent a text to my boss, I QUIT.

Freedom!

I also gave her the complimentary verity that the young fatso of a junior had been stealing off her for ages.

This is also true.

Have that you cow!

I felt as though I just got up, took a huge run and jumped right out of that plane that was causing me so much shitness and I was floating freely in mid air... But as with many things after impulse comes waking up the next morning. You land with a bang! To the voice that shouts... WHAT HAVE YOU DONE! YOU HAVE NOW GOT NO JOB!!

I sat in a daze, fuck!

Visions started to play in my mind. Questions start popping into my head. Will I now take part in joining the queue to sign on the dole and join the other jobless on job seekers? Where will I live? Will I have to live in a grotty bedsit somewhere? Will I have any money to buy food or shoes?

Great move I have now got no job.

Panic started to set in. Sort your head out my little voice said you are a stylist you have plenty of clients go freelance.

Yes I could do that, all I would need to do was tell my clients. I could phone them and tell them... What would I tell them? I thought and pondered over this for over an hour and decided that I will not be having any big majors, I was just going to have a summer off. I would now go to their homes, make them all look wonderful, life would be sorted.

I was sick of all this bullshit I wanted change, I needed change, and I had virtually demanded change so I accepted this change, this freedom, freelance it would be for me. Yes I can do this I thought. I then began the task of contacting my clients. I was going freelance.

Freelance to be free.

Most people where chuffed to bits when I told them I would now be cutting and coloring their hair at home, that I had finally made the move.

Others not quite as enthusiastic as me, not to worry I told myself, I will go back into a salon when the right position comes up.

What a fantastic summer I had, still working hard but to my own time schedule, I chose my own hours. I met friends for lunch, went out after work for a drink in my local, Sod that I was only allowed four Saturdays a year off I can now take as many as I like.

I went to festivals, I went to see live bands. I was spending more time with my family, my children. I met passing fling. I was starting to enjoy myself again. My life was getting good, but the longer I worked freelance the more hours I was putting in and the busier I became. I was having less and less spare time to myself.

I had told each and every person it was only for the summer, I had promised them, just one summer and I would then go back into a salon. And I would definitely be calling people when I do … As the colder weather kicked in and winter approached, my business had grown. People loved that it was me who got wet when it was raining and me who had to find a parking space and they would keep their new hairdo bouncy, I became the family hairdresser, but I had promised that I was just having one summer out of the salon. I started to think about which salon I wanted to work in. I couldn't fit people in for a fringe trim with five minutes notice or squeeze a client in anymore. I was working fourteen hour days so I needed a salon but which salon would become my master with me as their slave.

The thing was, being freelance, being self employed, my very own boss, gave me endless freedom, Hair @ Home… I had a mobile salon, a mirror and chair that I took into peoples homes, I had all the equipment, every shade of colour. My car boot became my stock room. I loved driving around in my car singing to music been able to nip here there and everywhere… if I wanted a extra day off, I took it, start late or finish early. Oh yes, I would now only have to ask myself. That is it I thought, no more bosses for me. No more you are only allowed four Saturdays off a year if you work in my salon. No bollocks to all that, I was doing this for me.

So I decided that maybe a salon of my own was the way to go. Carry on being my own boss.

THEN I MET HARRY

As I was driving along on my travels, going from one house to another, fixing my mind on trying to take the shortest possible route, so that I could make it to my next client on time, just for once I thought, I would like to arrive to a clients house on time. My time keeping was never that brilliant in the salon, it had become even shoddier than ever now that I was riding solo.

As I was speeding along hoping I would not get zapped by a cop for breaking the thirty mph speed limit. Out of the corner of my eye I spotted a sign, For rent - frigging heck I thought... No way... Wow, it was like a wish that had come my way. A big bright yellow banner that was sprawled across a shop window... FOR RENT.

I stopped my car.

'Wow, I couldn't believe it, look at that, maybe this is a sign. Yes, this is it, my change of life. I can run a shop', I assured myself. So maybe this is it...wow... It's not bad, not bad at all. The exterior looks in good keeping. I cannot believe it, good location, Yes. A good area for a salon, quite central, plenty of parking, all round winner. I might just give the number a call and see what is what when I get home I thought to myself. I wrote the number down that was advertised. My curiosity was telling me that it would not harm just to check it out. During the day I had started to convince myself I not only wanted but now I needed my own salon.

As soon as I got home from work I was already adamant in my head that the shop was now mine. The change, I wanted the change, I needed change, so this must be it, a salon. It must be a sign. I called the number and spoke to the shop owner Harry inquiring about the rent and various other outlays a shop would cost. Making no promises what so ever, as this was a big decision to make. I had to mull over the pros and cons, the fors and the against. Over the weekend I ummed and arrd, I changed my mind, I changed it back again and then I thought hang on a minute, what am I doing. Do I really want to be tied down to a salon? Tied down again after all these years, I have finally got my freedom. I can do what I want, when I want, whenever I want do it. I can do as I please and what with the state of the economy. No it was not a sign, now is probably not a good time to open a salon. Why have the extra pressure of having staff. No opening a salon is a silly idea, business is good. I then gave a little more thought about my previous plans, how I had wanted to have a summer off. I had a good summer, free, out of the salon although I did still put in quite a few hours graft being freelance.

'I want another summer off, a summer of freedom' I said to myself selfishly.

Business was good. Hard work but good.

I have had responsibilities all these years, I chatted away to myself, years of cleaning, cooking, washing clothes and the bloody school run. I hated the school run, we was always up late, if we had ran out of bread my two children would want toast, if we had bread but no milk they wanted cereals. I could never find a matching pair of socks. 'Wear odd ones' I would shout at the kids, 'just hurry up'. Never ever, could I find a bloody place to park, other running late disorganized parents also seeking out the treasured last parking space, I would spot an empty space out the corner of my eye, then I would put my foot down on the accelerator and swing my car into the space like a frustrated rally driver. To then have to jump out of my car, usually in the pouring rain and launch my beloved children into the play ground, who have not quite finished munching on their breakfast that they had to finish eating in the car, shit, they still had crumbs of toast or cereals stuck around their mouths whilst walking into the playground. I cannot send them into assembly with food stuck around their mouths and possibly a little snot. I didn't have a tissue, So quick thinking and sticking my arm up my jacket sleeve, I wipe each face with my sleeve. Then I would run like an Olympic sprinter going for gold back to my car, jump back in my car looking very similar to a drowned ferret and take off at break neck speed whilst trying to secure my seat-belt, trying but failing to get to work on time. Always rushing like mad, I arrive at work, late again all hot and flustered. I still have my children's snot and breakfast smeared up my arm, with hair looking like a bird's nest that has been left abandoned. I casually walk into the salon and I greet my first client who has been patiently sat waiting for me to arrive for the past twenty minutes. Eager for a new hairstyle, a new colour, hoping that I will transform them into some beautiful creation, to give them the wow factor, that extra boost of confidence. They want to relax and have a friendly chat, they do not want to hear about my chaotic morning. I apologize to my boss for being late again and I take a few deep breaths and put the hour or so of self creating stress to the back of my mind and crack on.

I soldier on, working my backside off. I mean five days a week Tuesday through to Saturday working from nine am until six/seven pm. sweating my ass off each day in the fish bowl that was salon life. Then after work has finished, I do not stop, I then set off for the evening shift, racing against the clock to pick the kids from after school care club to take them home. I then start again, cooking them their dinner, helping with homework, bath time then thankfully bed. Another day over and totally knackered! 24/7 I grafted hard to provide for my little darling off springs. To take them on great adventures, holidays in Europe, provide pack lunches, food, a roof over their heads, even the simple things which go so unappreciated, things you have to scream full force to get them to use... Tooth paste.

'Go on have another summer off' the little voice encourages.

Why not, I answered.

So I sent a text to harry explaining that I would not be interested in the premises. That I had changed my mind about opening a salon and that I enjoyed what I was doing. Thank you but no thanks. Somewhere from there I cannot say when, I ended up agreeing to rent the flat above. Not at first though, as to enter the flat you had to come in from the back alley and the flat was outdated, in serious need of renovating but Harry talked me round, promised that the flat would look wonderful, new kitchen, new bathroom with a shower, new central heating, he was going to make the place look brand new. Brand new and shiny!

Harry then came to my apartment to see what standards I lived in, to see if I would make a suitable tenant and with him he brought two different styles of kitchen cupboard doors for me to choose from, that would be fitted in the new kitchen.

From the word go... the little voice inside my head, kept saying something isn't right... *something is not right*... at this point I never really took notice of the little voice, Unless it said something that I liked. I did not like what the voice was trying to tell me so I pushed the voice to the back of my mind. I did not want to hear it. I was not the only person who thought the place had a lovely feel. My friend who had viewed the property with me also liked the potential. The flat, three storey was built over a hundred years ago, it felt peaceful, it had lots of promise, so I decided to ignore this little voice and made plans to move.

I handed over a large sum of cash for the deposit for the flat, the first months rent and for the legal contracts. A few weeks later, Harry put in plain words to me that he was having a few financial difficulties and would be unable to buy the new carpets he had promised. The new kitchen appliances and the radiators for the new central heating were already at the flat and as he had already started working on renovating, he was now half way through grouting the new bathroom tiles and had ripped out the old kitchen. I was determined that this was my fresh start and that Harry seems genuine enough, so without me even thinking about the possibility of anything going wrong, I then splashed out more money for new carpets and for the carpets to be fitted.

I went on a new home to be shopping spree. I bought a new washing machine, new light fixtures and wooden blinds for all the windows. I also paid for and painted the whole place as it was dark and gloomy, it looked really depressing. Every room had a different shade of brown painted on the walls and ceilings. I painted away like a busy little beaver excited to be moving home. The living room alone took four coats of paint, not cheap crappy paint I might add it had to be decent paint to cover the darkness… Yuk I thought as I slapped fresh cream over the walls. This was OK, for as far as I was aware Harry was doing his bit I was doing my bit. What could possible go wrong?

Harry had already given me a key to the quirky three storey flat and had allowed (oh the irony) yes allowed me to start painting. I worked my socks off painting in freezing conditions in Mid December. I was at the flat every single night after work to get it ready for my moving in date at the end of the following month,

I started a video diary a 'before and after' I was that excited, a south facing roof terrace that I must admit was one of the pulling powers that had me, as I was smoking a cigarette on a paint break, sat on the door step

33

looking at the moon, I felt a calmness, oh yes I was thinking how I could chill out here on a summers night, glass of wine, good book, just a chill place, somewhere to relax in peace.... oh how wrong could a person be!.

The morning of the move was approaching and up until this point I had started living again somewhere near happy land. I had recently experienced a death in my family and things had ended with passing fling -which broke my heart. I was extremely tired and I was coming down with a cold plus I had started to break out in peculiar rashes but life was picking up again or so I thought and I was kind of happy. Not quite fully smiling again after death but I was getting there. My busiest time of the year is December, everybody wanting to be all glammed up for their office parties or the Christmas festive celebrations, so I grafted seven days a week with late nights making peoples hair look wonderful. To then go straight from my last job to the soon to be new place and painting till early hours of the morning, singing along to the radio. I was proud of myself. I hadn't been round to what we will now describe as the squat since the week before, when I dropped a van load of belongings off with team A. The place was still not ready for a person to live in but Harry promised that it would be ready, that I shouldn't worry.

It never crossed my mind to nip round and check the place before I moved out of my apartment. I did not think that I would need to go and make sure that the place was in a liveable standards first. Who would? Harry was there the week before promising the flat would be ready for following week, I believed his promise.

The morning of the move arrived and everything at my soon to be old apartment was packed up. The gaff was pristine, cleaned top to bottom. I had borrowed a vac carpet shampoo hoover from a friend and shampooed all the carpets, a luxury penthouse apartment and very nice. I had lived there for a few years, all luxury apart from the balcony it was not worth having, oh did I love to complain, no it was useless you could not sunbath on it and it was way too posh to put a bit of washing out to dry. I then set off to my friends to return the vac, nipped to the shop bought a magazine and headed to subway for something to eat and a coffee and to relax for an hour to let the carpets dry, before collecting the helpers.

I was sitting down having a breather eating my breakfast thinking moving home is hard work. It had already been a long tiring morning packing the soon to be old place and that was just the start when my phone started to ring.

'Hello' I said happily.

'It's Harry there are a couple of jobs I have not managed to finish… I am really sorry… my wife has been taken into hospital'

'Is she OK? I ask

'Depression I think'. Harry chats on 'Just a bit of grouting left to do on the tiles in the bathroom, the kitchen sink needs plumbing in and the shower needs to be fitted… sorry… I thought I would have it finished'.

At that point I felt more compassion for his wife being rushed into hospital than I did for a couple of minor jobs.

Twelve pm the day of the move. I set off excited for the start of what was to be my new life, a new adventure. I drove around to group family members and friends who were my helpers for the day in house move number five. My family and friends I can safely say wasn't too keen on helping me move, yet they were there ready to help. Let me tell you that all my furniture is solid wood, bits I have collected from junk shops over the years, the posh apartment was a run up four flights of stairs… to posh to be able to put a few towels on the balcony but not posh enough for a lift!.. Team B was gathered.

I had arranged for a removal firm to shift my stuff but the man with a van was running late. I made a feeble attempt to keep the momentum up, to keep the helpers in good spirits and geared up ready to go. As they were all getting impatient and board with hanging around looking at the amount of stuff that needed to be shifted. When Andy the van man finally arrived, that was it, all actions go.

We carried stuff down the four flights of stairs, all of us working like the clappers, all chatting away, people who have not seen each other since my last house move. My spirit seemed to rise.

With the van fully loaded, and my keys to the apartment handed to back to the owner and a cheque given to me for the original deposit, I then set off the short distance, eight blocks away to the last hurdle.

We all arrived at my new home, I jumped out my car, walked down the small alley unlocked the security gate, climbed the stairs happily chatting away to my son, unlocked the door of my new home… horror! Oh my god. OH MY FUCKING GOD. OH MY FUCKING GOD YOU ARE JOKING!

The place was still a building site, nothing had been finished. A few jobs need finishing Harry had said... yep only a few jobs if you want to live in a shack in the middle of a jungle in Cambodia... The place was only just fit for a rat! And as far as I could see there were no rats running about, so even the rats had refused to take residence in this poor excuse for living accommodation. The radiators were still stacked against the wall.

I was completely mortified.

'The lying fat little tosser' I shouted, tears pricking at my eyes. I could not hide the look of shock horror on my face and I got the strangest feeling that I had just been zapped with a stun gun. Great stuff!

Harry had lied!

The place was not ready, nowhere near ready. I then frantically started picking, ha did I say picking, I started chucking all Harrys power tools into the corner of the room and started sweeping up all the crap from on the floor.

Where can I chuck all this rubbish? I cried. Whilst trying to create a little space to move my things in. I was in a state of complete disbelief.

I then discovered that my furniture was too wide to fit up the narrow stairs. So now we had to lift my furniture up and over to my new unfinished home, us trampling on the flat roof of next door home extension. I had now gone into a state of absolute shock. I was livid. I did not ask permission from my new neighbours to trample on their roof and they did not tell us to fuck-off, which was very nice of them. Lugging heavy furniture up and over to my new abode was major hard work. I was knackered, I was cured. This was not the kind of change that I wanted.

I could not believe Harry would think this place was passable for living in. In my head I started to fantasize that I was a black belt Thai kick boxer, who could swing my leg around and reach it thirty miles to Preeser and knock the fat fuck out... My day dream got me through the next many hours of mayhem.

As we were unloading the removal van it started to rain.. Great!

Thank you... this is just what I need right now.

Each helper was now trying to shift my furniture into my new residence as quickly as they possibly could, before it all got soaked.

We were now moving furniture in pure silence. The atmosphere was that thick and miserable it would need the blade of a samurai sword to slice through it. Great stuff, when things go right there right. When things start to go a little bit pear shaped, what can I say - It just had to rain.

Was I devastated? Yes, I would say I was. I believe I went in to shock. Was I angry? Oh yes, I definitely was angry. I rang Harry, all a bit of a hazy phone call but he promised he would sort things out after the weekend.

I needed a team C…

I was worn out and full of cold but with a new founded Team C and me, we set about trying to turn something crap into something less crap. I dug out my iPod, stuck some tunes on, opened a bottle of wine and we all got stuck in. With no hot water and no heating, team C worked away like first class troopers. Cleaning everywhere, moving furniture upstairs, and trying to reassure me that everything would be OK, they tried to help me see all was not that bad.

At about Three am I was done in, tired, pissed off, completely cured and cold. Team C left.

RELATIONSHIP FUCK UPS

A fter team C had left. I lit a candle and stared into the flame whilst lying on the sofa. The only little bit of warmth I had in the flat. I started to think about my life. What had happened and how the fuck did I end up here? I went deep into thought:_

My mind started to drift...

My career was something I used to passionately love; I like to think I was an artist on hair. A high-quality stylist, expensive but you get what you pay for, and I was very good at it. I loved it. Being creative was a passion. I enjoyed making people look their supreme best, with a natural eye for what suits each face shape and skin colour. That does not mean I fancy your man because I cut his hair, I am doing my job, which is to make him look his best. I see him in a black gown, under a spot light, in a mirror; I get to see all the imperfections. I cannot believe there is so much petty jealousy.

Being a stylist you do become close to the people you are making look good, you want them to love their hair so they do feel more confident. Look good- feel good.

Noxious the battle, the championship of the shit flinging mud bath that I had endured became a two year legal battle. I was fighting to keep my reputation as a stylist. My job had become my life; with the court case it gave me at first determination. To win, clear my name. With the shit that followed me around salon to salon I became disinterested in constantly trying to prove myself.

I had become friends with most of my clients. I would go into work early because they have something important on and they would need their hair doing or I would stay late because they had a home disaster. I never said no, not ever, nor did I ever complain. My children were then growing up, teenagers and they preferred not to hang out with me anymore, choosing instead to be with their friends. The children's father was still living in our home that we once shared so as the kids started to grow older they started to spend more time at their dads, to be closer to their school friends. They went to school in the posh area. I lived several miles away in a more affordable property. Their father was now at the top of his career ladder working less hours and I was fighting for mine, working more hours. The more my kids wanted to hang out with friends the more cash it costs. So the more I worked. People got used to me always bending over backwards that even clients would start taking it for granted. Friends just expected. Was my kindness mistaken for weakness?

Every day, all day I would listened to peoples relationship problems, medical problems, their children's problems and pet problems. I always remembered the name of each client and their family members name. I laughed with my clients. I always saw the funny side. I Grew close to some and I was surprised at the amount of clients that followed me salon to salon. Where ever I went they would follow. My spare time I would try to fit in family and friends and usually do their hair. Always working..

After moving around salons running from the shit, the mud, I didn't even need to use client record cards anymore. I could tell what shade of hair colour I had used before from just looking at my clients hair. It was like some little memory worker in my head ran to the memory saved file cabinets and grabbed out the relevant information and shoved it to the front of my mind. I gave advice when asked. I kept their secrets secret. We laughed at my fucked up dating disasters, my relationship failures.

My personal life was becoming none existent; I would always arrive to events late or cancel through working late either at a salon or in the clients home. In the end, I just didn't accept any invitations, then things changed and I no longer got invited. I had become the target.

When did it become that I was living to work not working to live?

When did my job become more important than my family life or my personal relationships? When did my job become more important than me? I wanted to be successful, independent, I wanted to shine, to have a career, financial security and only ever depend on me.

Sitting in the silence, mulling over the past, thinking about what I had now become. The more hours I put in at work, the more my own choice in men deteriorated.

All this shit, the mud that was slung in my face, teamed up with a few petty men and their injured prides, spitting out their dummies with their nasty insults and throwing their poisonous darts in my direction. My love life was really shit, on the surface it all seemed grand, but inside my heart had become hardened. I was unwilling to give any man my love.

The ice queen made from one disastrous relationship failure after another.

What is wrong with me? How is it that I can advise everyone else but my own relationships suck?

I carried on staring into the flame.

I had really wanted something to change. I had moaned and moaned; I had cast spells, said prayers, demanded and commanded change. I had taken great care in pointing out what it was that I needed changing. I had wanted this to change and that to change.

I looked at my plants 'Do you think that when I asked for change, this is what I wanted?' I said exasperated.

What is this? What is wrong with my world? This is the bottom of the shit tip!

How did I end up here? This is definitely not the change I wanted.

'My relationships never end well' I muttered.

The men you choose all have baggage themselves and you have now become emotionally cold.

Who said that?

You are In conflict with yourself. You want to be free but you also want to be in a relationship. You continuously rush along at top speed, too much too soon. Some men want to be hero's trying to fix you. Others are scared to death that you will have an affair. So they try to grind you down. The little voice in my head whispered. Some men don't like successful women.

I stared into the flame that was flickering in the darkness and drifted my mind back, thinking about my past relationships.

My first love. We had settled down and bought a house together, a posh house, in a posh street, in a posh area. The house was in need of renovation, we bought the house at the right time, before house prices went up massively and completely gutted the place. I loved my house, And then babies came along. I was still only a teenager myself. But I was happy. I had a new car instead of a wedding...I loved that car! We played happy families for the first several years. Me being a lot younger, quite stupid, totally naive and literally very dumb thought it would be forever. After the birth of our second child our relationship started to go downhill. I was now maturing and growing as a woman. First love changed, he changed towards me, he became distant and cold.

I ended up being trapped in a relationship with the worst control freak known to man. I would have spent less time in prison if I had killed him, but he is a good father to his children. I loved my home, yet I, myself was living in a prison. I was a prisoner in the posh house, on the posh street.

Nothing I did was good enough.

This man also had serious issues regarding if I would or would not have an affair.

Never! I used to think at the time.

'It is not if, but when with you' he used to snigger at me.

I was far too young to realize at the time that these controlling issues was because the controlling wanker could not keep his own penis in his pants. That he would place blame on me, accuse me of having an affair due to his own conscience of him being the cheat. No evidence was ever found and he still denies he had an affair when I was pregnant to this very day.

As a teenager I did not think that I was the most attractive woman on the block. I lacked confidence. My long hair was wild. GHD's were not invented and it never crossed my mind to grab an iron and stick my head on the ironing board to try and tame my frizzy horse's hair out. Plus I was not one of the lucky people who never had spots. My acne… I suffered with spots really badly on my forehead. I kept my fringe that long and my head down. I was lucky I never got hit by a car, or trampled on in the supermarket. I always looked at the floor. When I left school, I had originally trained as hair stylist but then babies came along and my own career had to get put on hold.

'doing peoples hair is not a real job, standing around chatting all day, mothers should be at home taking care of her children' Controller would say, informing me of this each time hair ever got mentioned, or if I was thinking about getting a job or having a career.

So there I was with two kids, a mortgage, and a man that worked away from home. I was in my early twenties and controller preferred it if I stayed at home to be a full-time mother. I loved my kids and wanted the best for them but I was completely board and mentally unstimulated, chatting to little kids all day waffling on about barney bear is not the best inspiring conversation for any adult day after day. Teamed up in a loveless relationship. I would dream of plans for escape but never carried them through.

I lived my life in accordance to his rules for years and years whilst my kids was small, although I did get myself a part time job as a sales adviser when my youngest turned one. Three days a week nine am until five pm, my children went to pre- school nursery.

My spirits lifted slightly thinking about how it was when it was just the three of us, me and my children. The posh house was miles and miles away from any family member or friends I had when I was growing up. Completely cut off. A different world from the council estate I grew up on. The neighbours were all a lot older than me and would snigger at the state of my house, trashed with toys, art work drawings that my daughter had designed stuck everywhere. Everything had a label attached to it, with what it was to help the kids learn how to spell. I had a wall knocked down to make a big open room for a play area with patio doors leading to a large patio area for toy tractor rallying. The front garden was grass for swings and slides. My garden gate was tied closed with a rope, so any visitors that arrived at my home would have to climb over the wall. The gate was secure so the kids could not escape, my son especially liked to make an escape for freedom whenever he spotted the rope untied. He would be halfway down the street on his tractor, peddling away, his little legs going like the clappers before I would notice he'd done a runner. The bigger he got, the faster runner I became.

I always had pots to wash in the sink, dirty clothes to be done in the laundry basket, piles of ironing. I was always behind on the house hold chores. Domesticated goddess I was not.

I was still a kid really myself thinking how I couldn't be bothered cleaning daily. Who wants to stay in and do boring stuff, it will still be there tomorrow. So when the sun was out we, my children and I were out. Staying in cleaning was not me that's for sure, no, I was off out with my kids having fun on the park or the beach collecting pebbles and shells, to bring them home, wash and keep them as treasures, and place them in our pebble basket.

'What have you been doing all week, the house is a mess' was usually the first thing he released from his grumpy mouth when he returned from working away, home only every other weekend. Both children then dumped me in favour of their dad.

Me being defiant 'I have been taking care of our children darling, what else would you think I would be doing'. The kids artwork paintings hanging up to dry, the dining table messed up with paints and crayons, toys scattered all over the house.

Being a young mum has its plus side, I could stay up all night when my baby was screaming throughout the night teething and still run around after my three year old the next day. I did not drink alcohol, not then. I did not party. I looked after the kids. I enjoyed colouring and painting with my children and did not giving a shit that my home was a mess. When the kids were in bed, I was alone. I read books, I played nintendo - super mario. - I lived a quite life.

Being with controller I was not too sure if I ever wanted to get married, well I knew that I did not want to marry him… Marriage is not for me I would say. I thought this was it for me stuck here, well until the kids grew up, this was my life with the controller controlling me… me being a true romantic that I was, I wanted true love with all the trimmings. Was I being selfish?

'You read too much mill and boom, romantic garbage, you should be grateful you won't get anything better' controller would gripe at me.

When I was stuck out in the back and beyond, cut off from my family and friends, left on my own to raise two smalls and trapped in a loveless relationship. Fantasies of the perfect man and how things should be ran wild in my frequent daydreams.

I wanted to be out of my life with controller. I wanted true love.

We were no longer having sex and we was not friends, we stopped hanging out together, the romance was dead, no more dinner dates, no more flowers, just sweet fuck all. Football was his passion so he went to all his team home games on the weekends he was at home. He would then spend quality time with the kids by taking them with him. Which gave me time out from the kids. As the years went on, as a couple we never spent any time at all with each other at all, we even took the children out separately.

I was glad to have a little break from the kids every other Saturday as their dad would be up with them, I usually slept till well past lunch time enjoying a morning lie in after being worn out from the none stop single parenting I had just put in. I was not allowed to go out with my friends. he controlled everything to paying the bills, the mortgage and to purchasing the main groceries. This giving him more control on the amount of money I was allowed. I paid the pre school nursery fees, which took most of my wages.

I would be better off without him I used to think, he could have the kids when he returned from the other side of the country. And I could have a life. I started to plan plan A. to leave. I started to secretly save all my spare money.

Oh how the controlling man wants to grind you down so you don't leave him. If he is that fabulous and every woman dream, why does he want to be with me? he would often call me a fat ugly turn off, or spotty features and tell me I was stupid. I was sick to death of his silent treatment when he was at home.

I waited till both my kids were old enough to understand what was going on, I then planned my escape to leave my house in the right location with my financial security. By now the kids were used to spending their time with their dad and me separately. After years of constant criticism, I had gradually over the years emotionally withdrawn from him. I got to the point where I couldn't stand being with him and I didn't want a affair, him and I was over. I was cured of his crap.

'You will never get anyone as good as me' he used to say, as if he really was the best I would ever get. The cheek on him! I wonder now with the fuck ups I've had if I made a mistake leaving but then I think no….no way. I was being emotional crushed.

As I started to grow as a woman and mature with age, my acne cleared and I started to blossom but I was becoming spiritually numb.

My wings had been clipped.

I started to became stronger more determined that I would not be controlled. I was not following my dream, I was in search of true love and happiness not put downs and criticisms. I left school with dreams, dreams of becoming a stylist., when I met him, the controller, I was working full time as a junior on a YTS youth training scheme and training to be stylist at a salon in town. I went to college one day a week. I was at the bottom of the ladder in my career path., with big dreams. My wage was low - shocking- twenty seven pounds and fifty pence per week. I would do peoples hair at home for extra money.

I qualified as a stylist getting my NVQ level two and started work as a junior stylist. I then became pregnant with my first child.

As the years went on and I developed more into a woman, confidence came along. Control freak then got even more pissed off that he was starting to lose his control and he started to criticize me in front of the kids. That was it. I was out of there.

I left the posh house in the posh street, my home I loved, when my children were six and nine years old, taking the children with me, I rented a property several miles away. Controller remained in the property we once shared, I drove each day to take the kids to and from school rather than moving their school to the new area we now lived in. The school run was now a twenty/thirty minute drive on a good day, moving didn't effect the kids, we remained as civil as possible during our separation-Moving out and taking the kids with me was a good move. I felt free. - the kids now had two bedrooms each.. The house I rented was a lovely little three bedroomed terrace. Controller was hardly ever at home with us, so it wasn't like they were used to seeing their dad everyday, and now having double of everything seemed to fill them with joy. I left my home in my search for true love... how young and foolish.

Was I foolish?

My children are now grown up. The days of school runs and holiday child care is now over. I am so glad I did things the way I did because the bond I now share with my children is tight, solid, it is real. They are my heart and my soul. After I left controller he had a promotion at work and was now coming home every weekend, The kids then went to their dads at the weekend, giving me more free time. When their dad swapped jobs and no longer worked away, the kids then decided at sixteen and thirteen to move in permanently with their dad. This shook my world. I was part way through my battle with noxious, It was strange living on my own but my kids were happy in their home with their dad. And their father worked less hours than me so it suited us all.

When I first left control freak there was not enough time in a day, to get through the mountains of washing and ironing, staying on top of all the dreaded household chores. I also had to work more hours, to pay the all the bills and rent, I struggled at first managing finances and having the added extra time consumer of turning into my children's private taxi driver, picking them up, dropping them off., my week was pretty busy. I never had any spare cash to go out that much. I didn't realize how much financial security I was used to until it was gone.

Lying on the couch in this freshly painted and new carpeted squat is not where I thought I would be, I said Staring at the flame that was now glowing brightly, swaying from side to side.

I stared and talked to the candle, the flame of fire…

I had still been under the control of controller for quite some years after I had left. Controller did not want any man around his children. That was fair enough.

'If you want a bloke, if that is what you want one see him at the weekends' he would warn me. I agreed.

I was still controlled by this man to go against what he said when it came down to the children. But I knew it was right what he was saying. I kept it separate.

After leaving everything I had in the search for true love, Controller refused to give me anything, it was my choice to leave so he financially cut me out. I had left him and our home so I never received child support but he did buy everything the children needed or wanted. I was more than happy with that, so I never took him to court for child support, me thinking I am better off being skint; we had food to eat and a roof over our heads. I was happy. I still had dreams one day to return to hairdressing and become a stylist in a trendy salon. I left sales and got myself a little office job and worked there part time during the week., nine thirty am til three pm, perfect at that time. I would then pick the kids up after school myself. no more after school care club at that time, which saved me money. My sisters would child mind for me in the school holidays. I did the usually mother stuff of taking them swimming and to karate lessons, if karate lessons was the flavour of the month. My kids never really stuck to sport or activities. My daughter tried horse riding once, dancing once, she just didn't take to it, she didn't like it, you cannot force kids. So I became a office girl during the week and then I worked on a burger bar Friday and Saturday night.

That was my life. I had the kids from Sunday evening six pm and not a minute past until Friday at six pm. Weekends I spent working, seven pm until five am and then I would sleep all day Sunday.

The smell of onions clung to my skin, what a crap horrible job but I needed the money and you have got to do what you got to do. With me being used to the controller controlling the finances I had no idea how to survive financially, cash, well it just burnt a hole in my pocket. It came in one hand and out the other. I did not have a clue on how to organize the bills or the rent. But I plodded along, I learnt as I went on and I did feel happier. I was happy, I was free. I was starting to work once again on regaining my confidence. I had no time for a romantic relationship and the lingering smell of onions was not the same as the sweet smell of Chanel number five. I did not smell anything like the sweet smelling sensation that would inspire romantic desire.

My thoughts of romance filled with passionate love making were simmered down. Although my dream was still there, all romantic mush that one day I would have happy ever after.

I am not sorry I left the posh house, it will always be my kids home. Just not my house anymore, I left... I said to the flame of the candle with a little bit more determination that I actually felt.

I had so badly wanted my own home again I cast spells for one, I prayed for one.

Now I am here squatting. Ripped off by the conman this isn't what I cast my spell for... I carried on with my thoughts, all mixed up -

I remembered some of my first dinner dates after leaving controller how nervous I was, how shy. A normal person I was back then sensible, rational, not psychotic, in a different land from lunatic - oh my oh my have I fallen from grace - yet I have no shame....

I was not too sure if due to my onion aroma that the men I dated were all slightly dodgy. I would go to the effort to get myself ready and on arrival at the restaurant I would be already thinking, no this man is not for me, that If I skip the starter and go straight to the main course, no dessert or coffee, just be polite as possible and leave as quickly as I can. And that would be that.

One guy before he got the courage to ask me on a date would bring me copies of music Cd's.

The music guy was lovely, a really nice guy and here he was bringing me music. Our date was anything but. This brought a smile to my face...a time when I was happy., I had no resentments or emotional pain. I hadn't experienced heartbreak, death or betrayal, I didn't know what a blackout was! I was guilt free. My once happy life…

The night of the date. Many many moons ago. I had finished work, collected the kids, sorted their stuff out for the weekend and at six pm they were now packed off, in the care of their dad. I started to get ready. Ready for my date. I had already mentally picked out my outfit during the day - I had thought about what I would wear all week, I even tried on different outfits in the days leading up to our date. The day of the date I had chosen to wear a floaty little chiffon black dress, vest style straps, just past the knee, I went for a classy look, teamed with a nice pair of black heals. So with the kids now gone I jumped in the shower and started rushing around to be ready on time, after I managed to tame my hair, blow dry and styled, I applied some makeup. I put on my dress and went to get my shoes from under my bed. My shoes were no where to be seen. Where are they? I was now throwing stuff everywhere, trashing my bedroom hoping they would turn up. Lovely was due to arrive anytime soon. I decided I better search my daughters room and there they were, my shoes…the toes now all scuffed. The state of them looked like my daughter had been bike riding in them. 'I do not believe it' I shouted out at my daughter even though she was now at her dads miles away. I took the shoes to the kitchen to give them a quick polish. I opened the kitchen cupboard and started searching for some shoe polish. I did not have any shoe polish just an empty tin… fuck…oh… I spotted that I had black shoe dye. Leave over night to dry the instruction read. Fuck it I thought It will be alright and with a cloth I rubbed the shoe dye all over my shoes.

Lovely arrived bang on time looking smart, he had definitely put in effort with his attire. We smiled, we were both little nervous. I did not know where we were going 'dress nice' was all he had said when I had accepted his invitation for a date.

We walked to his car, he had polished it, it was gleaming, and like a true gentleman he opened the door for me. He was sweet. I sat in the passenger's seat and looked around at the freshly upholstered vehicle. The power of the lavender air freshener he had used was overwhelming. The car must have stunk before, I was struggling to breath.

We chatted to each other as he drove us the forty minutes drive down the motorway to the city centre. We parked the car in a car park... wow I thought, I was well impressed with the city center and I followed him to the restaurant of his choice.

The city centre was buzzing with people. We walked along past the shops and the pubs, people with happy faces everywhere. I was feeling smart, sexy and confident.

We arrived at the restaurant, he opened the door.

'Ladies first' he gestured with his hand.

We walked inside and waited for the waiter to come over to us; I had a good scan at the place, looks good I thought, very nice.

Chinese, one of my favorites.

Lovely had paid attention to what I had said, what I liked.

The waiter came over.

'Table for two please' lovely said with confidence and a smile.

'Sorry sir, we have no tables left this evening' was the reply

'Oh' the shock on his face.

Lovely tried to barter with the waiter for a table but the waiter wasn't having any of it and carried on saying 'I'm sorry sir we are fully booked tonight'

'Come on, I know another good restaurant, the other side of town' he said trying not to let the slight error that he had forgot to book a table at the restaurant have me any less impressed...

We left the restaurant and headed back to the car. Where was the car parked? Which car park was it? Lovely couldn't remember where the car park was. We walked down the street and back up the street, up and down we marched whilst lovely tried to get his bearings of which street we should turn down to find the car park he had parked his car in. We sat down leaning against the window ledge in a closed shop doorway, my feet were getting sore, bloody heels! The colour in his cheeks was now draining from his face as he tried to rack his brains. He didn't know where he had parked his car.

I was gobsmacked.

Lovely then started to panic a little. I was a useless help, I hadn't paid any attention to what car park he had parked in, or what streets we had walked along. It started to drizzly, I then started to try and remember what we had passed. Lovely was in total panic. By the time we did find the car park and get back to his car it was lashing it down with rain, I was soaked and I was cold. My hair sprung out a extra few inches, frizzed out to the max. My under ware was showing through the chiffon and the shoe dye had now run all over and my feet. My feet were now stained black.

We sat in the car in silence, the smell of lavender kicking back in.

'Do you want to go somewhere else' lovely said not daring to take his eyes off the steering wheel and look at his water damaged date sat next to him.

'I want to go home' I said trying not to burst into tears, being as dignified as I possibly could. Slightly more chilled out than lovely because it wasn't my car that we couldn't find but I was still cured. No the date was over.

'yer alright' said lovely.

Driving back down the motorway, with the heat of the radiator kicking in drying us out and warming us up, I put some tunes on, he was now getting over the shock of losing his car and I was feeling a bit more confident now my dress was once again hiding my knickers. All the desire and passion I felt had been killed off by the rain.

He dropped me off at home and we never dated again. We managed to have a joke about our date, we had a good laugh.

The flame becomes hypnotic as I carried on in nostalgia.

So lovely was over and then I met and started to date a nice bloke, Mr snowboarder, he was sexy, cheeky and adorable, we dated for weeks whilst being all prim and proper, they are the rules in dating right? plus I was slightly nervous, I had very little sexual experience, so here we were getting to know each other only holding hand and kissing, building up the sexual tension, but when it came down to us getting groovy, shaking out a few moves in the bedroom. It was rubbish. I have never been so disappointed in my whole life, it was really rubbish. No sexual chemistry. This is not the true love I had been hoping for, I wanted spiritual chemistry, red hot to rock lovemaking, it was bizarre, we thought each other was hot enough to date but the bed wasn't rocking that night, sexual chemistry, the passionate desire didn't exist between us. What a waste of time! I felt awkward, unsexy, unattractive and dam right disappointed. Maybe it was my fault with the lack of experience I had, but even so. Now I am not sure how Mr Snowboarder felt, probably just the same. I figured I had wasted weeks of my life, getting close to someone for it to just fizzle out. Or maybe what I was searching for was true love, passion desire, lovemaking. I was expecting fireworks.

There is no point in a having a sexual relationship, if sex isn't right because then nothing is right. I wanted great sex with love. I had read about it. True love with a lustful divine.

So I had got myself into a bit of a dilemma. What was I to do? Was I to base an intimate relationship on just friendship? He was was tall and handsome, kind and sincere. What was wrong with me...

Friendship but without sexual chemistry...

Was I to settle for less. Of course I was not; intimate relations are based on sexual desire the burning flame of passion. The ultimate experience of the super dove! But you have to be friends also to make a relationships work. I wanted both.,

We dated for a while, things never improved. We then stopped dating.

I was full of Hollywood romantic bollocks.

If the sex is shit I might as well not bother I said to myself, why I would want to spend more years in a sexless relationship. I wanted some soul food, some passion to feed me orgasmic orgasms; I wanted spiritual and sexually chemistry, true love with a sprinkle of lust, to put the fire in my desire. I wanted some food to feed my soul.

After a few more dating disasters I met 'the one' he was tall, handsome, charming, sexy, polite, full on romantic. We shared amazing sexual chemistry we - I - could hardly wait to rock the bed, the couch, the dining room table, I fell in love, hook line and sinker for Mr Emotionally Unavailable. He was the one for me, he made me feel special but unfortunately I was his one of many.

If I had known about the other girlfriends that he had kept top secret at the start, I would have never have got involved. I would have never have fallen for his bullshit, I would never have allowed myself to fall in love with the lying cheating tosser, I told the candle. The flame bounced up and down.

By now I had quit the burger bar at weekends. Every weekend I was with the one, he would come and stay at my house, he would even bring his dog. The one who broke my heart.

By the time I discovered his deceitful ways I was smitten, in love... in denial. I couldn't believe this man who told me he loved me would turn out to be such a whore. A man whore.

Learning about his infidelities broke my heart. I was never told or asked if it was OK, that I was just to be a part of his menu and that I was simply a side dish, a little extra, him giving me nothing in return, a emotional conman, energy vampire sucking out my soul, he was getting my heart, my body and soul. I was crushed, sick to the pit of my stomach, I threw up. Was it Just sex to him?.

I would try to end the relationship but he would not leave me alone. He would talk me round. He would then try and turn things around by saying he did not want a relationship he just wanted us to be friends. 'I appreciate your honesty I don't want to be your friend. Now fuck off and leave me alone' I would yell at him

Be His friend!

Was this man serious?

He had not treated me like any kind of friend, he had treated me like a bitch, a sex toy, someone he could pick up and put down when it suited him. No matter what my dreams were for true love, the romantic notions of happy ever after were, this relationship was soul destroying. Should love not be a union of two people sharing intimacy, love and trust? My dream of true love was now at the start of being ripped out and destroyed. Is it too much to ask that my man remains faithful? He was a cheat.

Why did he want to remain my friend?

Can a person really remain just friends with an ex?

When I am treated with such lack of respect it makes my blood boil. He always denied the other women, until I read his text messages…

Tell the fucking truth I would scream at him, constantly pushing him further and further away. I no longer wanted this fucked up emotionally damaging pretence. Two people, who have seen one another naked, enjoyed each others bodies, shared sexual fluids, enjoyed intimate moment and shared the love. Was this all fake?

All this time have I been caught up in nostalgic bullshit? Was I being deluded, confusing lust for love?

If a relationship had started with sexual attraction and desire, friendship and trust, is that not how it should remain?

Does a relationship end because it didn't work out?

Was that what it was all about, was it just about sex?

I remembered how I got fed up with all the sneaky tricks, the lies, him making out I am paranoid. Paranoid, being a slight under estimation I turned into a private investigator, my bull shit detector was beeping. He is telling lies my little voice would say this isn't real love.

Was it around this time I started to learn how to read people? Read thoughts through expression and pick up on body language?

It wasn't the fact he was fucking other woman in the end, I was past caring how many, the fact that he had done it once was devastating. It was all his lies that fried my mind, broke my heart, he insulted my intelligence, he insulted me, he lost my respect, destroyed my trust with the verbal diarrhoea dribbling from his mouth.

Him being an innocent man and I am a psycho nut case for even thinking he could be cheating and screwing other woman. I knew I wasn't paranoid. I was mortified.

The way he became sneaky with his phone, the shiftiness of his body language. He was charming, sexy, intelligent but he was transparent with bullshit.

I cannot erase history and go from lovers to just been friends is this man for real? Is he taking the piss?

After the way I got treated, what a really crap, fucked up kind of friendship that would be. I don't want a friend like that.

Lets remain friends. What does that mean?

The one that has just been potted, dumped, is now trying to desperately cling on to the new "friends title" in the sad pathetic hope that one day he will change his mind. I do not want to live in false hope. If the relationship is over it is over, now do one, leave me in peace to get over your ass.

I started wondering what his motives were each time he would call.

What does he want?

Him using the clincher we are friends. 'I'm just checking if you're OK? He would sweetly say.

'Well' I say as sarcastically as I possibly could…

'Why would you think I would be OK you knob head, you cheated on me, broke my heart, now fuck off and leave me alone' A fight then starts to kick off between your head and your heart. Head stays in front…

Is that what I am now… grab a shag? Him smooth taking my knickers down with his cheeky sweet nothings when he is at a loose end. I don't think so. It does not take the sting away that I am no longer girlfriend, we are now just friends. And you would still also like to fuck me. Who do you think you are?

Lucky me, I cannot wait for you to screw my head a tad more. You get to break my heart, fuck with my feelings, play on my emotions and you expect me to be your friend and let you back in my bed! Not a prayer.

Fuck off!

Emotionally unavailable men can cause the worst kind of damaged a woman can experience. He will fuck you over emotionally, physically and spiritually, he will screw with your head. He knows the correct steps to get you to dance, he will do all the right things to get your love, he says all the right words, and once you get emotionally attached, your then fucked, for this vulture withdraws, then he comes back again, then he withdraws.

The more he withdraws the more emotional deprivation kicks in, your starved, leaving you desperate for emotional intimacy, making the once stable become needy and irrational. Mr E.U how he loves to disappear, then the silent treatment will start, you're confused. What happened?

He did not state at the beginning of the relationship what his true intentions were, as he is a selfish, self centred wanker thinking only of himself. He does not reply to text messages, he ignores call. This man has got what he wants. I would then try to get on with my life, start to heal, to pick myself up. For him to contact me, weeks later, he reappears with the same old bullshit that made me fall for him initially, he is charming, he tells you he cares. Bollocks, what a load of shit.

I now spent my spare time crying in bed, . listening to David Grey. The kids were a distraction during the week and kept me going but at the weekends when the house was empty, the loneliness, the heartbreak would kick in. I was heartbroken. My dream of true love and the one was now over, crushed. Never again would I let anybody hurt me, life became a daze.

How can a man like this care? A man who claims to love me, a man in love would not disappear for weeks on end. Popping in and out of my life, offering me his low grade friendship, he thinks will suffice for my love. A man who loves me wouldn't cheat.

My love is defiantly not blind, my vision is twenty-twenty. It is two people dancing together or I am dancing on my own.

He wanted his cake and to eat it. The voice in my head said rather seriously.

Was that it?

He thought that you will always be there for him, forgiving him, after all why shouldn't you forgive someone who has shattered your world, ripped out your heart and ditched it in the trash.

What a caring man he portrays himself to be.

Are you stupid?

This man is dangerous he wants to spare himself the guilt and remain your friend, but he thinks you are great in bed, a right good shag.

So he would still like the pleasure of the odd hook up when it suits his selfish desire, him being totally aware he is fucking up your world. The selfish bastard - do not fall again for his patter.

He does not care if he is hurting you, he is just using you, keeping his options open, whilst he is on the prowl for his next dating conquest, leaving you with your heart ripped out once more. When you know that when he is on the missing list he is having sex with other woman.

Hello... I am not your friend, you broke my heart, now fuck off!

Now I can understand why some woman would fall for this smooth talking sexy man. I fell for him, but I was not about to sell myself short and cling to the hope that one day he will realize how amazing the relationship was and maybe I would finally be his one!

Why would I want to wait around in hope?

Was it all in my head?

Not a chance that this will happen He will never be faithful the man is a rat.

This man will without warning turns up at my home wanting a coffee and a catch up. Looking delectably ravishing, turning the conversation into talks about the past; chatting on about the first time we made love. Is he trying to entice me back under his spell? You're left wondering what his game is, not trusting one word that drips from his mouth.

I am left thinking what the fuck!

Crazy thoughts thinking about the past, the bad memories, the amazing sex, how once I trusted and loved him with all my heart and soul.

A vicious cycle then starts of not seeing him for months and then out of the blue he appears again, like Houdini. at my home. I open the front door not prepared for his face to be peering at me, butterflies start flapping in my stomach, panic sets in, I am getting flustered, he has got a fucking nerve, what does he think I am his ego boost.

That after everything I would settle to be his little slices of pie.

What does this man want?

Could we be just friends?

Why can I not be his friend?

Don't be so stupid my inner self screamed out. Are you having a laugh do you want to be used and ditched again? Are you a total moron? Do you not have any boundaries? Do you not have any pride?

Tell him to fuck off and go away and to never come back again. Do not let him play with your mind, you don't owe him anything the man is toxic. What do you want to be extra nice, extra accommodating in the blind hope that he will do a big fat u turn, to return to how it once was. Wake up dream girl.

A door mat is something to wipe your feet on, not something you love and respect. My heart was broken.

I then moved into a bigger house, nearer to school for my kids, and I changed my phone number, all contact from the one ceased.

The romantic dream I had of finding true love was destroyed 'I will never give my heart to any man again', I would cry.

After "the one" I would spend many years in complete celibacy avoiding any potential development of intimacy, I didn't want to be with another man. My soul carrying the heavy anchor of the heartache. I was unable to let go of the pain.

My love, turned to hate. I hated him for breaking my heart.

After a few years the pain had been suppressed, buried in the cardboard box in the back of my mind.

My little pink wand, the little buzzing battery device became the only pleasure I required. A fantasy life safe from emotional harm. My imaginary friend from my lucid waking dreams became my lover.

'Do not make me a sexless spinster' my little voice would plead.

Sex verses love…

Had I wanted it all? The ultimate fairy tale fantasy; Friendship, respect, trust, love and great sex, was I asking for too much? the flame on the candle flickering as if a breeze was blowing directly on it. My thoughts were going deeper inside to the core.

As time went on and years went by my need for sex intimacy became stronger, life with a chastity belt on was frustrating and therefore some skin on skin action was to required, the touch of a lovers hand, lip locking, passion. I needed to blow away the cobwebs. A well needed sexual service to get the old cogs turning again, was required.

By now I was a lot older and I had returned to hairdressing. Starting at the bottom. I went back to college and attained my NVQ level three in hairdressing. I had worked hard working my way up from being a junior again, then a junior stylist and was now a senior stylist. I was married to my job, my career.

So I chose men for sex, friends with benefits, lovers. Am I a bad person because I wanted just sex? Human contact.

Two adults who are both willing to participate in the game of consented sex. Upfront and honest, no bullshit, no games, no strings attached. I did not want to date these men and I did not want anything more than sex, I still loved the man that broke my heart, I carried the hurt around like luggage.

I could not morph another human into the person that my soul wanted food from. I tried and it did not work I was in a loose - loose situation.

When did I turn into some kind of ice queen? When did I become so cold of emotion? A crazy woman, I had a few male friends with benefit throughout the years I liked them all, they were all good looking, good fun but not the one.

I enjoyed having a friend with benefits, I enjoyed male company, when I was to busy working and being a mother to have a relationship, it also covered the wound of heartbreak with a band aid. I was still pining lost love, friends with benefits is only a replacement, a temporary fix with no involvement, no emotions, friends with benefits comes with rules not to get emotionally attached. I would say...I am not in a loved up relationship... it is just sex, and it will not work if I daydream about it ever being more than it is, just sex. Yes he is good looking and good company but relationship possibilities they wouldn't get a look in, They didn't have what it takes, some men found this rather harsh that I was happy to to have sex with him but not date him, you have to keep a balance so no emotional attachment takes place.

Lovers became boring after several weeks or months. I would then resign from any male stimulation for a period of time, then meet someone new, a new toy to play with. Sex and love are worlds apart. Sex is great... love is special.

Love is not to be confused by lust. Love is opening your heart and soul. Love has no pride, love has no colour. It can happen anytime anywhere whatever your history, religion or culture.

Lust the tantalizing temptation, that starts out a sweet divine, can go cold pretty quickly which for me usually ended up bitter tasting. Followed by the dart throwing frenzy from the ex lover.

I had enjoyed the freedom of casual sex without the complications bit; I only used this as momentary substitution for love..

'I want to feel the love again' I sighed at the candle.

Releasing sexual tension in the form of having sex is good for the immune system. Play safe stay safe. But it is not soul food, that requires love. It can only be love.

What crazy wasted years. Wasted loving a rat.

During the fight with noxious, I was now working harder than ever before, incredibly long hours so I could save up for a barrister. In the first two rounds of the fight for what I call justice, I had no choice but to represent myself in court. I stood up against noxious barrister and won the first two rounds solo but at the final hearing I wanted a barrister of my own.

Like I say, I have never been brilliant with cash and although I was far from being in the poor house, I did well, I got to enjoy things in life... New car, nice clothes, going to good restaurant with my children, good holidays. I also spent well - I was financially ticking over month by month. I knew that at the final court date where witness would be questioned I would need legal representation, someone as good as noxious had hired. And good barristers cost money.

By now when I was not working, in my spare time I was searching the net for everything I could on Employment Law. I spent hours on end searching through the witness statement that my ex employer had based his justification to suspend me on and I went through these statements like I was removing head lice with a fine tooth comb, over and over combing out the nits. My living room became my office, I had typed out transcripts of recordings that had took weeks to do, listening, writing down then typing out. All in the correct legal format. Legal jargon piled up everywhere cluttering my space. Spending every spare minute reading the statements from noxious solicitor. Weeding out all the vast contradictions, the major flaws in each statement that my colleagues had written against me and they were plenty. The back stabbing bastards! Small minded people in our small town with their small little mouths that ran riot. Here was when the mud got slung in my direction I became the target, the victim of a hate campaign.

I had it in my head that when we had our final court date, me not being a trained barrister and not having any knowledge, experience or even bottle to stand up and question a witness in court, I would need proper help.

I barely had time to clean my home, I was in no position to commit my time to dating, so no strings sex/friends with benefits/ lovers, was the only available option. Uncomplicated natural remedy to totally distress, beats any form of medication or headache pills. If I was feeling achy through standing up all day styling hair or had backache through me being slouched at night at my laptop, or if I should start to get a headache through my mind working continuously, what better way to remove the stress and get a good night's sleep, friends with benefits… Some sexy hot totty for home delivery service. Saturday night take out. Nice massage, good sex, no feelings or emotions afterwards, just see you later, you can leave now. I would then take a shower, dive into bed, snore like the best, jump out of bed bright and breezy the next morning all happy and revived ready to carry on with life. My sleeves rolled up and ready to fight with noxious, with all my witnesses/ clients raring to go.

Good move on my part, With the surprising news that I had hired a barrister all of noxious witnesses then started to retracted their statements quicker than flies been sprayed with repellent. It was worth it as I won the case for unfair dismissal. The stress was over.

Does it make people feel like they are above everyone else being part of the demolition squad?

My thoughts were sliding deeper into the dark as I stared into the flame.

I wonder.

They were trying to demolish my life, cocky little bastards but not that cocky to get up in from of the judge. Trained barristers are like shit sniffers they know when you are chatting shit.

The little juniors that were so eager to be in this crew all writing their statements, encouraged by the owners and them being too young to fully understand that destroying someone living is fucked up – Making me a target for a hate campaign could have destroyed my life. It certainly tested my reputation as a stylist.

The lies, the rumors. The scum. I had two children to house, cloth, and feed when I first became a target And most importantly our yearly travels abroad.. Did they not think for one second that I would take their asses to court? Trying to ruin my life, my holidays. My reputation as a stylist. I do not think so.

Was I stupid to think that things in my life would now calm down a bit. That I would find the happiness I was searching for, with the court case now over, lovers got potted. And as I have said before, My children were older teenagers by now and living with their dad in the posh house on the posh street. I gave up renting a house. I first moved into a ground floor flat I only stayed there for six months, then I moved into the luxury apartment..

My train journey at this point seemed to be having another slight breather, my roller coaster ride of up and downs was temporarily at a station. Then I met my Ex.

Why did I not stay single?

Less hassle.

When my EX came alone. I was living in a penthouse luxury apartment and working in the salon. Life was good - No more court case and I was earning a decent standard of living, fifty - fifty self employed basis - mature career woman. Smart, Independent, confident. Nice car. I had it all.

Why was I complaining?

The human mud bath!

Suppressed emotional baggage.

Hurt, betrayal, broken hearts.

I really did like my Ex when I first met him. He was quirky. He was different. I thought this is it, he was attractive, funny, a nice bloke, he was romantic, sweet and musical, talented and smart.

He played by the rules so I played along too. He took me on dates and I waited until he asked me to be his girlfriend before I jumped to any conclusion. I had a happy autumn, winter and then spring dating ex, we went on holiday, we were loved up. We moved in together We split up.

Reminiscing I stare into the flame of light flickering in the darkness and carried on with my thoughts

Ex had always had temper tantrums, like most musicians can if he did not get his own way. We had briefly lived together the year before but he had moved into my apartment with me back then. When a burst of childishness came over him he would storm out only to come home again if all would be forgiven and nothing was ever mentioned again. This could be anything from a few hours or sometimes days. Ex had given his apartment up when he moved in with me but he would run off to his sisters when we had a row. The very first time we split up, the first time he left. my stomach sank. I felt sick. I spent the next five days of not hearing from him in a state of crapness. Over the coming months whenever we had a row and he left it started to get less painful. Then it happened, he started acting suspicious with his phone, making out I was a paranoid. Been there done that!

The day he moved out our local football team was about to play, to see if they could get premier status. I was quite at work on the day of the match, the whole town had gone to support our team. I came home from work early to find ex had gone.

I didn't mind too much as ex had left quite a few bits and bobs behind including his guitar This was not the first time he had moved out.

This day discovering that Ex had trotted off back to his sisters, he had left again, I was just not bothered anymore. Ex had already moved most of his things out. So when I came home from work a few days later to find he had been in and he had taken the rest of his stuff and posted the key under the door. I just didn't care. What a chicken shit he is I thought. During our time apart, I had quit my job and I had become freelance and over the summer months having time out of a salon enjoying my life, meeting my friends, spending time with my children. I was happy and content. I then met my passing fling, my voice said stay away my inner voice would not allow it.

Passing fling was just about everything I wanted sexual chemistry spot on. We danced, we laughed, we talked, we had similar interests. We chilled out together from day one and for the next six weeks we was glued like super glue. We would go to work and text each other constantly throughout the day - name that tune… with a few lyrics to go with it. We argued we made friends, each apologizing and holding our hand up if at fault, it was a refreshing change not to be always in the wrong like it was with EX. We both took a week off work, holidaying together having fun, I stayed mainly at his house- then it happened I got the text that he was falling for me. I felt the same. I could not be happier. Three hours later death in my family happened, my world came crashing down. I had arranged to spend the night with passing fling but stayed with my auntie instead. Passing fling threw a wobbler. Passing fling showed a jealous side that I didn't like. The next evening I met up with passing fling, our relationship ended. I was devastated.

Death freaked me out. I started seeing the dead! Lost souls everywhere. I could hear them, I could hear their voices.

Passing fling ended, crashed as death had arrived, I was in despair, the darkness had started to suck me in. I was being pulled in and out of the light. My business life was still sound, I held it together, my private life was falling apart.

One Saturday night as I sat in my apartment, drinking wine, the day had been a good day, I had worked hard, and was exhausted. I set off only to go to the shop and left the candle burning. Walking past the pub on my way to tesco express, I see a friend standing at the door of the pub 'pop in for a quick drink,' he shouted. I will I'm just going to the shop first, I bought another bottle of red wine. On the way back I called in, he bought me a drink we chatted, he left. I hadn't finished my drink so I took it outside. We had been taking about death, death was in the sky, I could see their faces, hear their voices, I started to cry. Then I started to sob - I started talking to the dead I could hear them in my head - I was asked to leave. I refused to leave our local pub - I was sat outside, sat at the table screaming at the sky. Crying - why. Seeing faces in the sky - clutching a bottle of red wine - They called the police - I was arrested.- I was barred.

My ex then reappeared back in my life and we arranged to go on a date, We went on a few more date. I became his girlfriend again and on what was a supposed to be a beautiful, crisp, Sunday autumn day we arranged to go on another date, what had started out to be a lovely morning, by the end of the day got fucked up, went completely off plan. The weather outside was cold, but OK, bearable, If wrapped up wearing a hat and scarf, with the sun that was sneaking out over the clouds. It was a nice day to get some clean fresh air. So it did seem possible that after such a emotional year, despite everything that had happened in the past, death, betrayal and broken hearts that things might turn out to be good.

I just carried on staring into the candle now thinking about EX.

Months had passed, lots had happened and here I was back with my Ex who was my boyfriend again, going on a date on a cold crisp yet sunny autumn day..

Ex was offering to pay for a private therapist. I looked like I was about to join the living dead, the comfort and support Ex was giving I confused for love. I was not really ready for a relationship but familiar comfort is what I needed. I needed to heal first, crazy thoughts had taken over my mind and I was an emotional wreck. I started seeing things, visions - ghosts. I started binge drinking on my days off. I was falling apart inside, being creative was not on the top of my agenda list, drowning my sorrows in cans of carling larger, sitting in dirty clothes, listening to voices chattering in my head, was more probable. People was now getting worried about me, all the true friends appeared, fair weathered friend could not deal with my change of character and departed from my life. I had been barred from my local and had been arrested. I wasn't to fussed, I did not care! I did not feel like being in a happy chatty frame of mind, being alone is what I wanted. Ex was supporting me. He loved me, so that was good enough right?

I was now getting ready for my date, getting ready for a night with ex, packing an overnight bag asking my guides for this and that. "No" popped up into my head, I wondered what the question was, I had asked that many, I need to learn patience.

I jumped into my car and set off to the shop; to buy some bits for later, wine cigarettes, munchies and on the radio was Annie Lennoxs singing... 'would I lie to you, honey, would I lie to you honey, now would I say something that wasn't true, I'm asking you sugar would I lie to you'... I arrived at the shop turned the engine off and got out. At this point of time I was still confused, was that a sign?. Did I just hear that, not really knowing the question. Is Ex just a liar?

I really did mean it when I say what a lovely day it had started out to be. I thought this was it, this time happiness. We had split months previous. I had an affair with passing fling I had experienced death. Here was my Ex giving love, support and familiar comfort.

I got back in my car and I drove to Exs

Ex was all happy and charming.

'Should we drive out to the country and have some lunch now' he said with a smile.

'We Cant, I have got an appointment at one, can we go after that, I am having another tattoo' I replied. I just thought I would pop round and see you first.

Ex wanted me to cancel the appointment, and spend the day with him but I had made the appointment weeks before we had rekindled our romance and there was a waiting list for the tattoo artist I had chosen and plus I wanted to have it done.

His features changed dramatically and he now resembled the look of man who had just had a bag of cow shit thrown in his face. His face distorted and twisted with anger.

I could not believe my ears. He is not telling me what I can or cannot have or done on my body.

My little voice chipped in 'I will decide what goes on my body thank you',

'I thought we was spending the day together' he chipped at me. 'We are just after I have my tattoo done' I said smiling at him. 'Come on I've waited ages for this appointment' I said.

'I'll be back in an hour or so, I wont be long' I told Ex, giving him a kiss before leaving for my appointment.

I refused point blank to cancel my appointment and went ahead and had my tattoo. This is my body I thought I will do what I like. Ex did not want to me to have a tattoo. I did.

I have to say I am soft and in my opinion I would state that tattoos hurt. They really do, unless you are rock hard- solid, a tough chick, unfortunately I am not a tough chick. I had been mentally preparing in the days counting down to getting another tattoo. When getting a large tattoo, the last thing you want to do is flinch on the table. This art is going to be a permanent fixture on your body forever, you certainly do not want to be a chicken shit and super sensitive and be crying because it hurts. You do not want to be yelling Arhh... like a big kid and pulling your body away from the artist, with the possibility of the needle zapping in another direction and you are left with an unsightly blob of ink, where a delicate leaf should be.

I was mentally ready and I had planned it, designed it, I wanted it, I was up for it... I was ready to go; I was feeling geared up and ready to inflict pain on my body.

We were shit as a couple the last times we were together I told the flame. We were more like friends, well at first.. No good as a couple, we disliked everything about each other in the end, our tastes were different, in music, in food, in the way we dressed. Our relationship was on, then it was off, then on again. Like a couple of yo-yos with the connection that wasn't real.

All bullshit and bollocks..

But here I was again with Ex, we was now back together. Was I giving him another chance? or was it him giving me another chance due to the fact my life had fallen apart. Death, heartache - emotional pain.

I was completely going against all the red flag and had over looked the small but major fact that I no longer found him sexually attractive. He is handsome but the initial spark had died. Or was I just dead inside. My spark had fizzled out for any man. I was happy when our relationship ended, when he left many months before. I had been freaked out over death. Had he homed in on the lowness that death brought upon me? Thinking she is down I have got her now?

The candle flame was jumping up and down in the darkness of the squat.

That lovely autumn day was anything but romantic.

Be with the one you love not the one you need my voice was saying in the background of my mind.

With my tattoo done I returned to Exs apartment.

We went out for some lunch to what was supposed to be our day. Oh hindsight is a beautiful thing,

'What was I doing?

Off we set, for our day out to have some lunch in a country pub on this sunny autumn afternoon. A pub I used to visit in my past, with the one. old memories came flooding back in my mind.

'Can we not go somewhere else' I asked

'Why the food is supposed to be good here' he snapped back.

He is in a man mood, great. I hate his man moods, when he goes all silent and sulks and I am supposed to over look any childish behaviour to keep the peace. It's like dealing with a thirty something teenager although far worse because you cannot send him to his room for time out. Ex was seven years younger than me maybe that was what it was.

I decided not to surrender to my bossy side and let him have his way.

I looked out the window at the country fields wondering if this man was right for me.

I do not want to go to this pub. I thought silently. The food is far from brilliant but best not to say anything, I don't want to get into a conversation of how do I know the food is not the nicest, best not aggravate his mood deeper and completely cure the rest of our day.

I carried on looking out the window and chatting to myself in my head.

I really did always need to tell ex out loud and very clear when something was bugging me, sometimes maybe more than once. I didn't want to upset Ex, so I remained silent. This day I just could not be bothered getting into a argument and maybe getting dumped and left in the middle of the country side. I did not have any money on me and was wearing heels so therefore I couldn't just march back home if I did get left stranded. With a bit of wise thinking I kept my mouth firmly shut. Plus I had yet to mentioned the amount of art work I had just had done. Like I said I did not want to get into an argument before lunch.

We arrived at the pub. And as the saying goes... half full or half empty.

That would depend on my mood.

My mood had changed from hopeful to new beginnings to what the fuck!

So now today the pub became half empty.

Even so the atmosphere was a boost from the icy atmosphere building between us.

The rest of the punters seemed to be locals, the regular Sunday lunch brigade. There was no back ground music playing just people chatting and the clattering of knives and forks, people munching away at their food. It was a small village not much else going on but this one pub.

This is going to be a bundle of fun I thought.

We ordered our food and something to drink and went to sit at the table over in the corner away from the locals.

We sit in virtually silence,

My tattoo started to get a little itchy. I tried to be appreciative that he had gone to the trouble of taking me out for lunch. It was a nice gesture but all I was thinking was what an ungrateful bitch that I am… was… I just want to go home rip this cellophane of my hip and butt cheek and get some cream on my new tattoo.

Please don't let it start scabbing I prayed, trying not to rip my dress off right there and then and remove the cellophane and scratch my body in front of the clattering locals.

'What is up with you' he asks in between mouthfuls 'I've brought you out for some lunch, you not grateful?'

'Nothing, I'm good' I said back with a smile.

But my tattoo was getting really itchy.

Him not being too keen on me having any more tattoos done and me not wanting to say exactly how much work via needle I had done, until he was in less of a mood and preferable at home.

If only we knew that this was what to be our final meal, our last dinner date.

Who knew that this country pub was to be our relationship grave, this quaint country pub with not much chatter, just the noise from the clatter of the cutlery between the two of us.

'Smile' I said clicking my phone camera.

Ex was not impressed with my Ansel Adams impression.

So I put a big smile on my face and owned up.

'Look, this tattoo is quite big' I told him whilst moving my hand around the area of my body the added tattoo now covered. 'its all flowers, flowers of spring' I told him with a smile.

I got the cow shit in face look.

'Can we leave? I could be doing with rinsing the ink and putting some cream on, it is starting to get itchy'

If looks could kill!

We finished our meal and left. Him storming out and me tottering after him as fast as I could to make it to the car before he had chance to get in and drive off leaving me stranded.

When I was sat securely in the passengers seat I took a deep breath and thought that went down like a lead balloon, I best be nice.

On the journey back, we hit bad traffic and we was stuck in a jam. All I got from the broken record that was his mouth was 'do you not think that tattoo is a bit too big? I told you I didn't want you to have one done, did you do that to piss me off?' he was going berserk. Pissed off already and now he was getting road rage.

'No I had it because I want it' I explained

He is not that impressed the little voice said.

Well he will have to get used to it, I cannot wash it off and I love it, he shouldn't be flattering himself that I would have a huge tattoo done just to piss him off. What is it with some men?

We arrived back at his place I took my dress off, put a tee shirt on and smothered my new body art in cream, poured myself a glass of wine got Ex a beer and sat down to chill out.

Ex was that pissed off about my body art that he was now refusing to look at me, he put a movie on, then he fell asleep.

Relaxing or should I say I was trying to relax, lying on one side whilst trying to let air breath on my freshly needled skin. I poured myself another glass of wine. The movie was rubbish so I flicked on the TV. As I was watching Come Dine with Me, my mood lightened the commentator is hilarious and you can get some good cooking tips, I looked around at what was to be my life.

Do I want to be here?

Do I want to live here?

I felt something strange like this wasn't it, this was not my destination. I felt at ease-ish, happy-ish, comfortable-ish, my life was having a quick power charge. But I felt like it was not quite yet over.

There was more to come.

I was mulling things over in my head. Ex wanted me to move in his apartment with him and he was to charge me.

I would pay him rent, we would not split the cost like most normal loving couples do, no, not with my Ex, I would be no more than his lodger.

I was just not sure.

He was to charge me more than half, more than he paid and for that I would get a key and a double wardrobe, *a key! Did this man expect me to wait outside for him to arrive home or was I supposed to be eternally grateful that I was allowed to let myself in!* And cable TV. He had sent me a list of the conditions a few days before via text. No shit, this was his agreement. I was expected to keep the apartment clean at all times. I would only be allowed my children to visit, no friends and for that I got the honour and the privilege to spend my life with him. And sleep in his bed.

'Is this the right path?'

I was now asking my guides.

I decided that when I was going to ask a question to my guides, instead of thinking it would be like sending an instance text message to whomever. I started to imagine writing my question to my guide in a letter, putting it into envelope, taking the envelope to the post box, hoping royal mail would not decided to go on strike, wait patiently for my letter to be delivered, crossing my fingers that it would be read and then wait for a reply.

I turned my attention back on to the TV and drank more wine. Ex started to wake up.

What happened next was far from normal loving behaviour.

What had my relationship turned into?

Was it different now? Was I about to take his controlling bollocks, now that I had been ground down by death. Was I going to cave in and start being told what to do, by a man?

More than a decade had passed since I had removed the one from my life. All flings had finished. The court case was over, but death and betrayal had arrived. I felt I had no time or energy to invest in a relationship and all relationship are about timing, are they not?

So was Ex just a comfort, support in my darkest time?

After 'the one' if I thought i got the vibe something dodgy was going down I would never confront a guy till I had hard evidence. I was now a bit more astute and went with my instincts.

Sussing out Exs face book account password, the last time we was together was easy, I do not know how I knew it but I just logged straight into his account and read his messages. I did this a few times before I told him and gave him the right to change his password. I was wounded, not crushed or devastated, life carried on as usual each time he went missing, off he trotted to sulk, to slag me down, to bitch about me on face book to other girls not woman, young girls, how sad, how tragic.

I already know before I looked, what he was up to, from past experience. Been there done that. You don't just say 'hey I was just wondering if you are seeing other woman, I know you live with me but things look rather dodge and I would just like to ask… That conversation is never going to take place…

He will not tell you the truth, he will lie making it far worse because for some strange fucked up reason I already know.

I read the messages he had sent slating me for chucking him out again – she does not deserve you; come the flirty reply to his inbox.

Now how the fuck does this chick know what I deserve?

I deserve a flipping honest man who does not go behind my back flirting or insulting me. I was hurt.

For him only to want to come home/back again... oh how the wonder returns but only on the condition that all would be forgiven and nothing was ever mentioned again. How could this be?

How can I not ever mention the fact that the very man who expresses his love to me, goes behind my back and slag's me down to young girls and then he wonders why I get mad. Are men totally stupid?

Could it be that your childish behaviour and the insecurity that you have a balding hairline be reason for your need to have secret woman friends, sugar coat the space of where your insecurities rest, to boost your ego! What am I daft?

Ex said I was just being paranoid. Was I being super sensitive towards to his much younger secret female friend?

Storming off all the time can be draining to a relationship and like I said his disappearance act would last anything from a few hours, sometimes day's then it turned to weeks then one day he was gone.

All bullshit and bollocks.

Well back to the day...

I was thinking about how kind Ex had been since death, how understanding and compassionate he was now being towards me and forgiving me that I had had a relationship with passing fling after he had moved out. We had spent months apart maybe this time it was different maybe he really did love me, maybe this is as good as it gets.

And he had forgiven me for having a relationship with passing fling, five months after he had walked out. He had left, we were over, I was free to do what I liked. But I had now been forgiven.

Ex woke up after his afternoon nap in a mood, again, just for a change. I had forgotten about his moods.

He started chipping at me, then we were chipping and bitching at each other. I was at his place. I had been drinking wine so was unable to drive and he had nowhere to storm off to. And I cannot throw him out of his own apartment. Ex thought it was some kind of defiance that I had had a tattoo. He did not like that he had said no and I had one anyway.

Wind him up my little voice said see what it would be like if you had a disagreement on his turf.

We chipped and we chipped.

'Get the fuck out, go home' he snarled

'Don't be stupid, I have been drinking' I answered.

Storming round, he carried on shouting at me.

'Go on, get the fuck out'

'No I am not walking home at this time of night' I snapped back at him. 'I have been drinking wine and I can`t drive'.

'Get Out'

'NO'

He was stomping round the apartment in and out the living area like a ram on a wild frenzy.

How dare you refuse to leave he is not going to like that, little voice said.

I started Laughing at him 'You have got nowhere to run off to, have you, I can't go home, I cannot drive, I'm not walking home in the dark' little voice had popped right out of my mouth.

He couldn't run off, so I started to tease him. It was a novelty to me as I had not ever seen him not be able to walk out. I wanted to try and calm the tension in the air plus I was over the limit,

'Nowhere to run to baby and nowhere to hide' I whispered half singing. Hoping it would lighten him up and he would recognize the song.

What he did next was a totally shock.

I am still to this day gobsmacked.

He called the police.

I was devastated. I had been arrested when I was hit with death but that night I was lost, I was lonely and I was scared.

I sat on the sofa and watched him dial 999 asking the police if they could remove his girlfriend. At first he wouldn't give my name, then he looked at me and he grinned as if to say your fucked now… I just shook my head. He then told the police my name, they asked him questions he LIED, she has punched me in the face and has busted my lip, and she is in a violent rage. I could not believe it. He then ripped his cold sore from his lip, blood started to dribble down his mouth onto his chin. I was yet again gobsmacked and unlike last time I got arrested, this night I just went numb. How could you do something like that, you fucking vicious wanker.

When he put the phone down, I said to him 'I have done what, you lying fuck' I was calm. I sat down.

I sat heaped in the kitchen waiting for the police to arrive. I wanted a sign I sighed. I did not want to be arrested. 'You know the drill, calm down pull yourself together and wait for the police' the little voice soothed and calmed me.

I knew after my last arrest how it would be.. I would be spending another night locked in the cell.

The police arrived. Two riot police, they were big fellers let me tell you -I did wonder if they sent them after my last arrest drama - this time when they arrived I was very calm, very rational. Blood was now pouring from Exs lip. I was arrested for assault. I said nothing. The policeman carried my bag as we walked to the van. The policeman first opened the van door then he cuffed with as much discretion that he could. They saw I was different from my snot tears and tantrum the last time I was arrested, when I was screaming my head off and was thrown to the ground and cuffed and then had to be slung in the back of the van, that time the van charged round at every corner chucking me around like a rag doll in a washing machine. for me refusing to leave my local. No this time was different. The journey to the station was pleasant if you can call been cuffed in the back of a police riot van pleasant. I was calm. The van then stopped. They then took me out of the van and booked me in, told the sergeant that there were no signs of damage as far as they was aware. I then removed my jewellery, handed over my stuff to the desk sergeant, who then wrote out an itinerary for my possessions and the police officer then led me to my room for the night - a cell.

The cell was getting cold, all you get for comfort is a thin piece of foam wrapped in thick blue plastic, I put the end over my feet... why didn't I bring socks?, oh I know I was not expecting to spend at night in the cells!.

I sat in the freezing dirty cell and I started to evaluate what the fuck had gone wrong when I had set off on my journey to find true love.

What went wrong in my choice of men?

Why do I attract men who want to control me, to change me, cheat?

I left my posh house in the posh street in search of something in search of love.

Had I sold myself out?

Was I on the wrong path?

'Yes I do think you are' said the voice.

Am I the only person that one day wakes up and think this is it, I have had enough of the good stuff – time for change, to jump on to another train… destination destruction…

Was I being that ungrateful that I had turned down his offer of going to live with him, we had been spending time together we were sort of getting on?

'He was taking you for a muppet', voice chipped in, 'A real first class muppet he wants a lodger not a equal relationship, someone to share the rent, ease the pressure of the bills, a live in cleaner who he can shag, who pays him for the privilege, you have a good deal there… A hundred pound per week and that gets you a key and double wardrobes do me a favour'.

Why that is an offer one should not refuse, hey lets go and live in the mansion, he has rules.

The next morning I was taken for my photo shoot looking surprisingly better than the previous time. I would even push the boat out and say I looked slightly healthier. I was thinking thank fuck I look half decent this morning…the police officer told me to look directly at the camera - I didn't smile. After a night on a stinky mattress you look absolutely stunning…Not! Having trying but not being successful at getting any sleep, whilst being freezing cold lying on a stinky mattress in a stinky cell. Then the officer took me to be interviewed and to be charge with assault.

Clever me - for I had snapped a picture of Ex at the relationship grave and was able to show the sergeant a picture taken the day before, with the big horrible cold sore he had in the corner of his mouth, I told the sergeant that he had ripped the cold sore off and lied about me hitting him, I had not hit him. He had picked his cold sore.

The police statement said it did not seem that there any signs of violent outbursts, nothing smashed ect ect… nor any resistance from me and I was released without charge. I was grateful as after my previous arrest the caution stated that I had to be a good girl for twelve months.

What a fucking liar but another dart was to get flung in my direction. More lies, more judgement.

I meditated and prayed in the cell that night.

I could not deal what was going through my head. My heart was broken. I did not want to meet him the night of death because I was dealing with shit in my head…

THINGS GO BAD TO WORSE

tried my best to get some shut eye. I tossed and turned all night but here I was now living in a squat. Sleeping for me was just not happening. Thoughts were whizzing through my mind. Old thoughts, forgotten thoughts, the painful memories. I became numb. All I could do was stare into space, so I would avoid having to clap my eyes on the mess that surrounded me. My mind totally confused, the darkness was now changing into mid morning light.

Looking up at the freshly painted ceilings, for what seemed like a life time. Thinking about how I had spent many hours painting it, to remove the shitty colour of paint. I was starting to get even more pissed off when I looked at the new carpets I had fitted in the living room and bedroom, I thought about all my relationship fuck ups and wondered if I wanted a relationship again.

I don't think I do. I have tried love a few times now and I don't think it is for me. I grumbled.

I got up and went into the kitchen to make a hot drink, a hot drink of something I thought, anything just to warm me up. I looked around at the building site I had just moved into that was now my new home wondering what the fuck have I done.

Yesterday morning I woke up in a luxury apartment. This morning I have been awake for more than twenty four hours and I am now living in a shit tip that is this freezing cold flat.

'Thank you, this is just great' I said to the universe. I grabbed the kettle and go to the bathroom to fill it with water, seeing the cold air depart from out of my mouth and turn instantly to frost. I then march back to the kitchen, sit the kettle back on its base and flicked it on. Whilst I was waiting for the kettle to boil, I started searching for the coffee, rummaging through the boxes marked kitchen but I could only find tea bags. Now that is just bloody typical I thought... I am not unpacking, I will buy some more coffee because I am not staying here, I declared to the cold empty squat. I made myself a hot drink, looking around at the unfinished kitchen.

I was cured, I mean really cured, I was extremely tired, had a snotty bright red nose and was cold. I hate being cold. What is going on?

'What the fuck is this place?' I inquired. Clasping my hands and pressing my fingers around the warm mug of sweet tea to feel the warmth penetrating, as if my whole survival was dependent on it. What was I thinking handing huge amounts of cash over. I was still in the state of absolute shock just wondering about the place, wondering how I am going to survive living in this unfinished dump. When there was a loud knock at the door. 'Who in their right mind is going to want to come and visit here' I said making my way to the front door.

I opened the door and see Harry. I looked at him and see his face drop, his jaw dropped down bounced off the step sped back up and cracked him right back in his face. His face then appeared normal again. Did that just happen?

Harry looked totally disgusted with himself. I looking horrifyingly in a state of full blown shock, with a resemblance to someone who had just been knocked down by wagon, in a hit and run the day before and was just shuffling around here until I realized I was dead.

Harry was standing at my front door holding a Hoover and a bucket with what looked like cleaning products crammed into it. Stood behind him was his teenage daughter who looked noticeably more pissed off than me, that she had been dragged out of bed at the crack of dawn on a Sunday morning, to come and help her dad clean my three storey shit tip of a flat. We both stared at each other for a brief moment.

'We have come to clean' Harry groaned at me...

I glared at the Hoover for a brief second then I imagined smashing the Hoover round his fat horrible head and said as calmly as I could possible muster;

'Clean?'

'Clean... I do not want you to come and clean, I want you to bring an electrician'

Then I slammed the door shut and stomped around fuming. 'Does harry need a head check? Does he think he can run a hover around and hey presto I will have hot water, or a bit of ditto spray will suddenly make my cooker work… I have no heating…the prick'. 'I have already got a hover and cleaning stuff… I've already cleaned the place myself… I need an electrician and a heating engineer' I seethed in anger as I marched upstairs.

The weather was now below minus degrees. The coldest month of a long wet miserable winter. I was freezing,. It was freezing outside and it was freezing in the squat. Not quite the quirky flat on three levels I had imaged up in my mind when painting, when my vision was I would have gas central heating, with a brand new kitchen and bathroom. That picture I had in my head had just been ripped off the wall, thrown in the bin and disregarded with the rest of the rubbish.

I then started to try and shift things around, the stacked up laundry bags full of clothes and unopened boxes piled everywhere. 'I need something to keep me warm I am cold' the little voice in my head said, so I started rummaging through the bags and bags of stuff to find something to prevent me getting frostbite or worse hypothermia.

Too much stuff and too much shit everywhere.

Finally I manage to find my daughters ski jacket and a sleeping bag. Result I thought putting the jacket on and wrapping the sleeping bag around my shoulders. I looked around and felt shitter than all the shitness I have ever experienced before. Right fuck it, that's it I decided, where am I going from here? I wanted change, I had asked for change. I did not want this I shout out, this is shittier than the shit. 'I want a house' I screamed to the universe. 'I want a house' I then prayed to the big guy in the sky. 'I want a house with a garden' I say to my statue.of hear no evil.

'I really am not staying here' I told the universe halfheartedly. 'Not a sniff' I then left the rest of the boxes which contained my belongings in untouched. There was not a chance I was going to unpack although I could not unpack even if I had wanted to and I did not want to. There was no room left for me to build my wardrobes or my bed anyway as Harry had left all his gym equipment at the flat. He had said that the equipment would be moved by the time I moved in. Harry is a conman said the little voice.

The room, my new bedroom now had water dripping in, snow was now piling high on the roof above. Getting more annoyed and feeling a lot more disappointed, deflated and ultra depressed, more than I had ever experienced in my life, I decided the best thing to do was to take myself in the ski jacket wrapped in the sleeping bag downstairs and watch some TV. Cheer myself up; watch something that would help lift my spirits. As I felt my spirit was slowly starting to have the life sucked out of it. I was slowly becoming one of the living dead.

Back in the living room I started to shift a few things round, I dragged the TV stand over to the corner to the plug sockets, I started to feel a little more cheered up with the thought of watching a bit of telly. I found the box labeled remotes and leads and dug out the ones for my TV. I put the TV on its stand then I put the roof aerial connection into my TV. I then turned on the TV. No signal`. I then tuned the TV to find the channels and waited for it to pick up a signal. No signal found appeared on the blank screen. I do not believe it. I could not believe it. The TV aerial was duff, broken, useless.

That was it I rang Harry.

'Hello Harry, I got another problem there is no T.V aerial either, what have you let me move into?' I said with poor hatred for the fat little man.

'Your TV must be broke it worked fine for the last tenant'

'No my TV is fine; I have checked the aerial with my bedroom TV and the aerial does not work'.

I marched outside and looked up at the roof. Again I could not believe it there was no TV aerial, none on the roof, not one which I could see. But I was not crying my heart out this time. This was the final nail, the last straw, no fucking TV.

'There is not a TV aerial Harry, I am stood outside I can see on the roof and there is no TV aerial. Who in the right mind in this decade, really I mean, really decides that they are definitely not ever and I mean never going to watch the telly, when you hang out and are chilling at home'

I ended the call.. I was fuming, rage steaming from my ears, the kettle that was my head was now starting to boil.

I was angry at myself at this point for not checking things out properly in the property. For handing over cash for the bond, contracts and the first months rent, carpets and fixtures.

Tears were trickling down my face and I paced around the cold bleak soul destroyer of a flat. Wrapped under a sleeping bag and zipped in a ski jacket. Isn't this life just the best!

After pacing around for some time and demanding to the universe I want out. I want out, I WANT OUT NOW. I then calmed down, I sat down, I relaxed and I meditated.

Well that is that I said to myself, there was nothing I could do. I did not have a TV aerial plus even if I managed to get a TV aerial, I did not have any roofing ladders and even if I did have a aerial and roofing ladder it is not likely that I would be climbing up any ladders. My energy levels were at zero I could just about conjure up enough energy to drag my ass off the sofa to make a brew. There is no way anyone would be climbing ladders tonight not with the ice and the snow on the pavements, no not tonight. See what can be done tomorrow.

Great!

So with no TV -No TV aerial. I would not be watching any Earthquakes, heat waves, sandstorms, bomb raids, Alien abduction or any other tragedy that was taking place around the world to make me feel better. Instead I thought I will just sit here and freeze to death, in the silence. I was now feeling in a very sorry state for myself, completely mortified, but not screaming for change. I was now starting to think about what it was that I really did want to change.

I dug out some more candles and lit them. I stared at the flames for hours and hours on end. Watching the light flicker in the cold silent darkness in the isolation of the squat. Looking at myself, my life, what did I want? Where was I going from here?

I was not; I mean defiantly was not that thankful at all, that I had a roof over my head.

Dear big man in the sky thank you so much for giving me a roof over my head.

I was ungrateful, a brat I did not want this toy anymore was my new favourite tantrum. Thank you I have got a roof that leaks all my boxes of things are now going to get damp.

Too much shit to move anyway, you do not need it all, little voice said.

What could get worse, what could possible get worse? I thought, nothing could be worse, what could be worse than this!? The fact I have just spent a small fortune moving into an unfinished flat and I feel ill. I look like shit, and I feel like shit, life is really shit. I am cold, hungry and I am tired. I have got no bed and I cannot cook so tell me what could be worse? I ranted, at the universe. I had no energy left to scream I was screamed out.

Then it hit me I had just spent a small fortune to move in to a squat; I was here, this is real what could be worse!?

'What could be worse? Do you really want to know?' the little voice said.

I came of the squat with the intentions of going to my aunts to have a warm shower, some hot food and to watch a bit of telly and was about to get in my car. I looked down at the wheel of my car. Fucking great stuff! my car had been clamped. That is just what I do not need right now! In the excitement of moving into my crap squat, I had forgotten to tax my car. 'Do traffic wardens drive round searching for cars at night? Do they get a bonus in the pay packet fucking someone's plans up?' I ranted ripping the sticker off that had been fixed onto my window screen.

The next morning I dialed the number and spoke to the clamping firm. A bloke answered the phone. 'You have to come to Blackhorn and pay one hundred pounds first thing tomorrow morning' he said. Clearly not giving a stuff that my life was already filled with enough shit. So to get the clamp removed I would now have to cancel all my appointments, ring a friend to see if I could get a lift to Blackhorn the following day and make sure I was up nice and early to buy a new tax disc for my car. So I could then show it to the man in the office and I had to do all this before he would arrange to have the big yellow clamp removed from my car.

Bad luck... It seemed like I was constantly getting bad luck, a flat tyre or parking tickets. The more I moaned the more bad luck started following me around like a bad smell and my skin was still covered in weird peculiar rashes and dry skin.

Ask for when will things get better, the voice said.

I burst out laughing the voice had now become soothing.

'If I had decided that I was going to squat, which I never would have chosen to do' I said back to the voice 'realistically though, I would have chosen a better squat to squat in. This place is shit even for a squat. What was I thinking? I would have chosen somewhere that had at least the minimal of a coal fire. I could buy coal to keep myself warm and turned it into a make pretend camping stove and heat food up... future planning' I said a bit more chirpier than I actually felt.

So here I was, squatting with no hot water, no heating, an unfinished kitchen with no cooker with a completely useless bathroom, with a toilet that you cannot flush due to blocked drains and live wires hanging out of the wall over the bath where a new shower was supposed to be. Not that it made any difference what so ever that the shower wires was hanging out of the wall. I did not have any hot water to run a bath.

Weeks passed excuses came.

His wife had gone from depression, to her having a mini brain stroke and then she had three more mini brain strokes. After the mini brain stroke whilst in hospital they had discovered a hole in her heart. Poor woman I thought, with the slightest bit of compassion. I felt a bit ashamed of myself for ranting on about having no TV aerial, no cooking facilities, no heating and no hot water. I was still cold and life was really shit.

I was still in shock and my cold was turning into flu.

I called a friend Darrel… I did not ask for help. I pleaded in-between sobs 'can you' sniff 'fix my flat' sniff sniff. "Pleeaaase" sniff, sneeze and sniff again. A damsel in distress! Ha it was not quite that story where the prince comes to the rescue the beautiful princess trapped in a castle. This prince was coming to rescue the princess from the dead. The living dead on Dog Shit Alley that would describe me a bit more spot on. I looked and felt like I had been buried two weeks earlier and now I had just been freshly dug back up.

Team D arrived. Darrel and Simon to sort out the million jobs that needed to be done but mainly the plumbing under sink, connection of my washing machine, install the shower, fix the ancient immersion water tank and connect the hob and cooker. I was hoping for the basics really.

I was looking forward to this day, kind of like a child looking forward to Christmas, where it is already known that Santa would be fetching an x box that included a selection of over a hundred games. A plasma TV fifty inch surround sound, complete with a big comfy games chair- leather reclining, a brand new mobile phone with a free contract and a season ticket to pizza direct with the number on speed dial.

Darrel and Simon arrived and walked around the flat.

'Put the kettle on then' Darrel more of told me than asked.

So off I trotted and went to make both fellas a brew. Hurrah I thought the rescuers are here and they are going to sort my flat out. I am going to have hot water and to be able to make fresh food. I was overcome with relief; I am going to be saved. With each of us having a cuppa tea in hand, I then walked the lads around the squat, pointing out what jobs needed to be done first. Both men were a bit more than stunned by the state of my flat but more so by the state of me 'god you look rough kid, you alright' Simon asked me.

'Love life' I said as animatedly as I could.

Simon and Darrel poked their heads around everything, all the doors and the cupboards. They checked out the light fixtures and plug sockets. Every time they looked at something they laughed. My stomach started to sink. I mean they just burst out laughing then they both looked at me.

'Why the hell did you move in here?' Darrel stated.

'Harry my landlord was supposed to renovate the property before I moved in, he promised me it would be finished by the time I moved in' I told them. 'I am so pleased that you came to help and made me feel three zillion times worse, please fix stuff' I virtually cried at them. Tears started welling up in my eyes, standing there wrapped from the freezing condition, with my clothes and ugg boots on, also my dressing gown over the top for the extra layer, topped up with my ski jacket and then doubled up with a sleeping bag, wearing my hat and my gloves. I was shaking with cold and feeling incredible dizzy and light headed. Whenever I stood up, all that I wanted to do was to plonk my backside down again anywhere I could and sit right back down. It was just as if I was about to faint into my coffin, and peg it, cold stone dead at any given moment.

'Look at this' Darrel roared out loud in a burst of laughter.

Simon made his way back downstairs and over to the kitchen sink, the washing machine could not be connected.

'No way, you are fucking joking?' Simon gasped.

There was no hot water pipe, again I could not believe it, it did not have a hot water pipe not in this under the sink unit, completely standard in most kitchens but none in this one. The cold water pipe was there but it was lead and a lot thicker than it was supposed to be so without an adaptor was absolutely useless, so my washing machine couldn't be connected, but no hot water pipe, not that any of us could see. I had to check for myself just in case the lads were winding me up. I had to double check and I wondered why on earth had I not made sure that there was a hot water supply for the kitchen.

All kitchens nowadays have a hot water supply do they not? Or am I one of the posher people who expects, that when I rent a property the kitchen includes hot running water. Yes, that must be the reason I had not checked half the things out in the flat. I expected! That was why I had not checked all this out before. Silly me!

I had also expected a TV aerial, How stupid of me for taking these basic things for granted. As I felt the temperature of the kettle in my head raise. I breathed in slowly and deeply letting my stomach fill with air, I then slowly breathe out, in and out. In then hold, both lads just stood there silently witnessing me going into another mini pre shock which has sent me plummeting straight back in to shock.

'So' I say to the lad's still half breathing out. 'To now add to the jobs of things that need to be done, the flat also needs re-plumbing?' Burst of laughter came from both of the men.

'Great' I cried. My stomach sank.

Simon and Darrel both refused to touch any of the jobs that needed fixing at my flat, not one!

I begged and pleaded for them to at least get the cooker working – 'no cannot do it, sorry' was their answer. I wanted to stop them from leaving. I wanted to jump in front of the door to keep them in… This is a siege! You cannot leave I would say whilst plonking my backside down at my front door but before I could drag my ass over to the door, they were already half way out. So then my instinct was to grab their jackets and pull them both back in and force them to stay, keep them both prisoners of the squat, locked in slavery until I had a hob, no not just a hob until I had hot water but off they trotted, chattering away to each other about what they would class as such poor workmanship. 'Unbelievable cow boy work, we aren't, we can't start touching any of that we would then be liable' Simon told me.

'Yer sorry - Not a chance we gonna put a finger on that' continued Darrel. And Team D left.

By this point I really did feel like saying fuck this I have had enough, the game is over… Where is that coffin!

Christmas day as a child this was not. This was not what I wanted. I wanted stuff fixed, this was a shit Christmas.

I called a few more friends but nobody was prepared to repair the damage to the botched up cowboy job Harry had left me to live in. Every one who turned up to look at the squat had said no there was nothing they could do, that none of the work would pass a safety test. But they all agreed on at least one thing and that was the flat was dangerous.

So Instead of the big fifty inch plasma TV and an x-box 360, complete with all the trimmings. What I received was operation! Not even a new one, the board game I got on this pretend Christmas morning was shit and second hand with the edges of the box tatted.

Buzz electric shock!

I did not feel right, I could hardly move. Walking from the living room to the kitchen was a massive effort. My aunt had brought me round a bottle of covorna cough medicine, by now my cold that seemed like flu was definitely more than flu and was starting to have me over. 'I don't feel well' I moaned. I crawled back on the sofa, adjusting my ski jacket and pulled the sleeping bag over me and drank the medicine like an alcoholic on vodka numbing the electric shock.

What more can a girl want!

At least I have a roof over my head, I told myself, albeit one that leaks but a roof nether less.

COUNT YOUR BLESSINGS - Up until this point in my life I never realized, it had never crossed my mind, on how much lack of compassion for other people I actually had. Distractions from my normal routine of every day living in my little life, my silver bubble, that keeps one consumed in their own little bullshit world. Made up of shit and yet more shit. Problems, I thought I had, well they were not really problems at all. Life before was not really that shit, I thought to myself. I looked around at the squat I was now living in and thought now this is shit. Had I been taking all the things I had all around me for granted... *I want a washing machine, a cooker and a toilet that flushes!*

High ho high ho, it is off to the launderette I go as I cannot use my washer as it cannot be plumbed in... High ho..... with three sacks of washing that needs to be done High ho.... Again I counted my blessing, that I did live in Blackrod and that there is a launderette around the corner. I started imagining what it must be like to live Ethiopia. I would never, I mean I would never have been able to carry this load of washing on the top of my head and gracefully walk down to the stream with the other African woman, to scrub by hand and wring out all of my clothes, the bedding and the towels and to do it without the aid of any washing powder, that gives clothes the smell of freshly washed laundry. Nor would I have been able to carry or even drag this load of wet washing back to my shack to dry. I counted my blessing again that I could take my washing for a service wash. I huffed and puffed and dragged the bags from my car to the service wash. 'Wash and dried please' I said to the lady behind the counter. 'Not a problem' she replied and handed me a receipt and off I trotted back to the squat.

By now I was getting really pissed off with my new living arrangements. My son on the day of the move had bailed and bolted back to his dads. He was quicker than a rabbit on amphetamine to get out of the dump that was now mine. Who could blame him, I couldn't, not with his dads alluring home that was softly singing in the air … Come and stay here….the house that had a warm fire and hot food, a comfy bed and a TV. It sounded like paradise. I am coming with him I wanted to tell his dad.

So I decided that now after all these weeks stuck in this sorry excuse for a home it was the time that I would have to mention something to Harry. Did I say mention? It is better if I said when I phoned Harry I screamed hysterically like a two year old having a massive tantrum. *I cannot stand it, I have had enough, I want out.* I am not living like this. I will not live like this….. We live in Scotland in the Twenty First Century not in a flipping third world country.

The squat was starting to grind me down. I was by now having to get myself up extra early each morning. That task alone was pissing me right off. To have to get up and get dressed, to drive to my aunt so I could take a shower. I started to sleep in the clothes I had on to save time and then drive a few miles down the road, so I could take a shower at my aunt's house. All this before I even set off to work. I could not cut somebody hair with armpits that stunk of body odour. This new routine every morning before work was getting to be a right pain in the backside. I was never organized, never on time. I was always trying to play catch up, always running behind, dashing off here, there and everywhere.

I was struggling to get off the sofa, let alone add any extra hassle to my day, by having to get up an hour earlier. I started thinking maybe this flu is more than just flu. I was drinking cough medicine like it was fresh orange juice, who needs a spoon when you can just take big gulps straight from the bottle and I was popping all in one flu tablets like jelly tots. My diet became really poor with no cooking facilities, jam butties and cup a soup were on the menu for breakfast, lunch and dinner. I was becoming increasing more and more tired, constantly drinking red bull for energy. I was completely knackered, drained. I was being sapped of life. It was impossible to get a decent nights sleep crashing on the sofa. My sleeping pattern was becoming back to front. 'I want a bed and a shower' I complained to the universe. All a person wants to do first thing in the morning, when they wake up is have a coffee and to jump into the shower. Their own shower they do not want to get dressed, drive a few miles in rush hour traffic to only have to get undressed have a shower and then redress. Again I was being extremely grateful and at the same time thankful that I had a car, as to walk the few miles each day in the cold and the rain would be a right proper bummer.

Harry came up with more and more excuses they were by now rolling of his tongue like a champion bowler knocking all ten pins down in one. The lies varied in extreme from little porky pies to big fat crackers. No little coughs or flu like symptom that I was suffering with. No not with Harry's bullshit excuses. These were serious, life threatening illness. His whole bleeding family seemed to be getting diagnosed with something different every other day. His wife had had three strokes or was having heart surgery or had a kidney infection. The lies came pouring in. His wife was in a right poor state of health. Then it changed to his father. He then had to visit and take care of his cancer ridden father. 'Today might be his last day' Harry would say. Then his daughter she had just became epileptic and he had to care for her and feed her. Harry came up with different stories but the more and more lies he told, the more he got himself mixed up and ended up looking like the fat lying little twat that he was. What next, let me think… Will you be called up and stationed in afghan to fight the war. Can you produce medical evidence of all this bollocks? is what I really wanted to ask.

The cold and the silence, was OK for a few weeks. Well it was nowhere near OK it was very far from OK, it was horrible. By now it was getting curable, I *was* cured. I was unable to get myself warm. I was cold and my stomach felt empty, starved. I started to think about the homeless people and with it thanking my lucky stars that I was not getting my head down for the night in an old smelly sleeping bag, fenced for protection with a cardboard box, residing in Blackrod bus station. Oh such happy thought were creeping into my silence and so another hour passed with me thinking that if I was homeless, I would hope to be one of the lucky ones and that someone would have donated me an old sleeping bag and a cardboard box, so I would have some type of protection against the wind and rain during the night.

Red Alert! Red alert!! Patience running thin! Getting very thin, it's running out... SNAP.

Snap crackle and POP... patience it now has gone...

I phoned Harry 'I WANT OUT, I WANT MY MONEY BACK'. I shouted my demands. I am living in squalor, I am living in a dump, this place is not ready, it is not safe and I am frozen. I cannot eat properly and I have got no bed. I cannot keep going to shower at my aunts house, now I have spoken to solicitor -saying this sounded so much more threatening than I have googled your greedy ass -

And you had better sort it out..

After my outburst Harry agreed to sort the squat out.

I was then shipped out with a bag of clothes and some toiletries, to go and stay at my aunties, so my home what I now describe as the squat, on dog shit alley was finally going to get sorted.

Going back to live with my aunts was like going back in time, it was good for a short stay, she rocks as people go, but I am a grown woman who likes to live life my way which means I like plenty of peace and quiet and I had been used to living in silence. I like to come and go as I please and wash the pots when I want, when I feel up to it. We liked different programs, we had different sleeping patterns. We are different generations. It was nice to get up, shower and go straight to work. It was nice coming home from work to a warm house. It was nice being with my aunt. I started to feel slightly better health wise. A warm house and good food is just what I needed.

I received the text from Harry a week later 'flats done' was all he put in his text. Both I and my aunt were cuffed to bits that the flat was finally ready. Brilliant. I text him back asking is it ready for me to move back into today. Then it came... just the TV aerial and the drains to do. It will be sorted by Saturday.

Only two things left I can live with that so I gathered my things, hugged and kissed my aunt and moved back into my flat.

My friends and family had started to lend me DVDs something watch, to take my mind off sitting in silence; I just stared blankly at the screen.

My aunt and me, we always had a thing we would do when something is good on TV, a good documentary, of phoning each other and letting each other know the time and channel. My aunt phones me to tell me that there is a great movie on later I will defiantly like she said. 'I've still no TV aerial' I would say. My aunt would then roars with laughter proclaiming to have forgotten.

As I was sat watching a DVD, thinking yes life could be getting back on track. I received another text message from Harry, saying he wanted me to sign a new contract. And that he was putting the rent up a hundred pound per month. I replied straight back - You cannot do that. No way am I paying any more money. I have just signed a twelve month contract, I have paid the rent, I was living in squalor for the past month and at my aunts. I am not, defiantly not going to sign anything else. Harry then sent another text 'As I have spent over a thousand pound on central heating you will pay some more rent into my bank account by Friday. I will give you the opportunity to pay by Friday or I will turn your electric off'...

What? What do you mean you will turn my electrics off? He is not allowed to do that, that is against the law. I tried to report Harry the con man to the police but as I do not have any small dependant children they refused to do anything about that certain threat.

I text Harry back that I had only just moved back in two days ago, I am not paying any more rent and a thousand quid for five cheap convector heaters that are practically useless. I could of bought them from Homebase and plugged them in myself and the cooker still does not work and I was still without a shower. Then I fired off another text- what happen to the gas central heating that was supposed to be installed, the radiators were against the wall originally. Click something went...what was that? The lights, my DVD and TV went off. No he wouldn't? He has, the twat has put a pound coin meter in anybody got a pound?

I jumped up and ran to the shop, changed a note for some pound coins ran back home and inserted a few pound coins in the meter. What an ancient meter I thought as I turned the silver dial to let the money drop. I haven't seen a meter like this before... I put just two of the convector heaters on, my new central heating system, in the front room and kitchen and went back to the movie and started to chill out. A couple of hours went by then click. Everything again went in blackness, bloody heck I thought that doesn't last long. I put in another pound then turned the heaters off and crawled into my sleeping bag, put the duvet over me and I tried to get some sleep.

I got up in the morning, made myself a coffee turned the heaters on. Switched my laptop on and logged in to read my emails, after about an hour. Click.

For fuck sake this meter is going to cost me a small fortune I thought. I put another pound in, had a wash and went to work. When I came home the whole place was in total darkness. Did I leave something on I wondered to myself, no surly I didn't. I definitely had not. There was nothing that could be left running. I put another pound in the quid munching machine and checked if I had indeed left any heaters on. No nothing running whilst I had been out apart from my fridge. The meter had chomped the quid and the only thing on was my fridge, Surly a fridge doesn't take up more than a pound a day does it?

Well how much does it cost? I asked myself. I put another pound in and I flicked the crappy heaters on to take at least the chill from the place away. Then I checked out the pound munching meter to see if it had some kind of manufactures details on it and then I began the search on the internet for electric RCD meters and the average cost of a unit of electricity. Click… gone again.

I cannot afford to put this bloody useless heating on I thought digging back out the ski jacket. This meter at this rate will force me to become a bank robber. I will have to raid the bank across the road. I will have to do something if the weather carries on like this. I was not shaking this cold off and the meter is munching pounds like obese folk munch Jaffa cakes. Now that is well planned out bank raid Maggie I told myself, the only gun you have got to your name is one for a silicone tube and I'm not too sure the bank girls would take the raid seriously and hand over a stack of pound coins. I laughed at the prospect of raiding a bank with a tool you use to seal the edges of a bath with.

Sunday afternoon my daughter Susan returns from travelling around Thai Land. 'What a shithole' she said as she slung her case on the floor. 'What possessed you to move into this dump?'

'Don't ask' I tell her. As we were sat chilling together, trying to get as comfortable as possible in snow jackets, snuggling together under the sleeping bag, watching the DVDs I had been given. I say we were chilling we were more like half frozen corn on the cobs. The convector heater took the room from frozen to chilled and with not one of us being daring enough to venture out in to the colder zones – unless we had too - out there behind the door of the front room. It was freezing out there, we both would be buzzing and finding it incredible funny if either one of us wanted to go to the toilet. You need the toilet yet? I smiled at my daughter, 'Nar! I'm gonna try and hold it in a bit longer, I think', Susan laughed 'it's freezing out there!' Knowing we would both end up laughing and running to the toilet like Linford Christie and jump back under the sleeping bag as fast as we could.

How nice it was to have her back home from her travels, maybe life would get less shit I thought. I missed laughing, I was miserable on my own all the time in the squat.

The thousand pound state of the art heating, the convector heaters that were inadequately useless was munching away money, the cost of running them was driving me nuts. Just as we was getting to the end of the movie Click!

I got up, I was pissed off again but tried not to show my anger, I had already put five pound in the meter that day, as my daughter felt the cold, from just returning from a hot country and here I was putting another pound coin in. But when I inserted the pound, the meter didn't click; it did not registrar the cash. Fuck and shit I don't fucking believe this. The electric did not come back on. Oh shit shit shit, so I put another pound in... Still the electrics did not come back on. Just Great!

I just love sitting in the dark, it is my favourite past time, it is just the way I love to spend my evenings relaxing. I really was not pleased. Then I remembered Harry threat, no surly he wouldn't of? Would he? No he can't! He has, he has turned the electrics off. He wouldn't of I said ... oh yes he has the little voice in my head said. This time I listened

In a complete fit of rage, I text Harry - very funny put the electric back on – Harry did not reply to my text or answer his phone, so I text again – I will report you to the police unless you turn the electric back on - about a hour later all the lights and the heating came back on 'I cannot believe he would do that mum' said my daughter. I did not go into all that had happened since I had moved to the squat, now was not the right time to dissolve her happiness, with my sorry story of being conned so soon after her fantastic adventure...

'Well he switched them back on now' I said as calmly as I possibly could.

I was pissed off to the maximum now, life was shit but this was getting to be unbelievable, the cheeky fat little con man I thought I have had enough of you..

As my adult child slept at the other end of the sofa, I decided that I would dedicate another one of my evenings on the internet googling ways to cheat an old RCD money meter. Good job I have a pay as you go dongle! - We cannot live like this, constantly frozen I said to myself. I am gonna find a way to slow down that bloody pound munching machine. I cannot have my child being cold. Even if she is grown up, she is still my child I said out loud so that it would justify any cheat I might find. For the next few hours I surfed the net looking up RCD meters and if there were any cheats. Just as I was just about to give up and admit defeat that you cannot cheat the pound muncher, I stumble across a forum about the old RCD shilling meters.

Well well well… my whole body lit up with delight. I went on to read how people cheated the meter in the forum posts; How when the Lecky man came round to empty the meter, no rebate was given just bits of crap, what this dudes mum had put in to tie them over… Mmm… I thought, let's see what it registers.

I jumped out of my duvet and braved the North Pole weather condition that was the temperature in the rest of my flat, leaping around looking for my savings money bag, rubbing my hands together one to keep them warm and two I felt like a cartoon thief.

I was that relieved when I eventually found the money bag that I thanked God. I went back in the living room and I emptied some of the contents on the floor and started to see what fits: 1p nope, 2p to big, 5p nope, 10p to big, 20p… BINGO. I emptied the rest of the bag and dug out every 20pence piece that I had, then carefully and slowly filled the pound munching machine with as many 20p's that it would take to fill it up. Oh yes turn that heating on. I was chuffed to bits. I felt happier than a pig rolling in mud! I wondered if Neil Armstrong felt this good when his toes touched the moon….GET THAT HEATING ON FULL.

THE ERRATIC ELECTRICS

N ow this was the beginning of what was the start of my landlord thinking he was God by flicking the electrics off constantly.

He would turn them off. I would go mad he would leave me with no electric for what seemed like hours on end. I would be left sitting in the cold and the silence.

I had nothing to do but be left with my thoughts.

This it is not my idea of fun!

It was now getting completely right on my nerves, I had developed flu again and it had come back full force. I looked like crap and felt like crap, I did not want to drag myself anywhere. I mooched about in the freezing shit tip with nothing to do but think. He would then turn electrics back on... This game became quite boring after a few times, kind of like playing patter cake with a baby for hours on end. Harry was insisting that he wasn't turning them off;

HELLO ... you are not going to admit turning the electrics off now are you, as that is against the law.

I decided that I had had enough. My health was rapidly deteriorating so I called the environmental health team at Blackrod County council. A lady came out to inspect the property and she looked absolutely stunned at the state of the place, although it could have been a disguise for the shock at having to see the state of me greeting her when I opened the door.

I was now a self certified Covorna junkie.

I do not think people really believed the shocking standards and I mean shocking standards of how I lived. I could tell that the lady wanted to leave as soon as she arrived. Who would want to visit here? Who would want to live here! I would not be here either if I had the choice, I was by now missing work or changing peoples appointments. I did not have any energy left to go outside let alone to move all my belongings back out again. My belongings still remained packed. And I had signed a twelve month contract. I am cold and I am hungry, please find out what can be done, please get me some kind of standard of living. I am still unsure what I am doing here myself, I said this out loud although it was meant more for my own ears.

In council ladies thoughts I could tell she was thinking "suicide watch".

Council lady was frozen cold in nine seconds flat, however she still managed to give me a warm little smile. We both then marched around the place checking for any proof that Harry had rented the place out in an unrentable standard. The lady then called the fire brigade to come round and conduct safety checks as there was no banister on the open plan stairs. The council lady took quite a lot of photographs and noted things down on her clipboard. By now she was trying to rush things along as her warm smile had vanished and she now looked like she was about to slap me around the face, for bringing her to the squat. She looked cold, she was wearing only a shirt and a thin blazer, her hands had turned into a glowing colour of red. The fire men arrived and noted that quite a few safety regulations had been skipped and that building regulations were not up to standard.

A few days later I received an email from council lady with an attached copy of the inspection report. Council lady had given Harry eight weeks to sort the place and fetch it up to basic living standards.

Bonus I thought, this will cost the fat little man more than a few quid to sort this shit tip out. Council lady also wanted to inspect his other properties. Let us hope there not all like this then he will be sorry, little voice said.

Now that would be the proper thing to do, the right thing to do, when a landlord rents out a property he should make sure it is habitable and safe. Or so one would like to think, so I do not think I was going beyond my rights here. Harry had to sort the squat out and provide me with a few basic essentials that were to include; a toilet that flushes, yes a toilet that flushes. It is disgusting having to shove poo down the loo with an old mop. I also wanted a cooker that worked and a hot water supply in the kitchen and adequate heating, the basics really. The heating Harry had installed was a bag of shit! He was now also to provide fire alarms and to re wire the security lights outside were also instructed.

All jobs Harry had promised would be done when I signed the contract.

I don't want to be falling up the concrete steps in pitch black at night or to keep having to use my mobile for a guide light, it's dangerous. I mean really dangerous even danger mouse would be slightly scared walking up that narrow concrete staircase in the dark. The list was endless with other major jobs like repairing the dangerous electrics, jobs that had to be done.

Tuesday morning all the electrics went off, patter cake patter cake bakers man, slap Harry round the head as hard you can!

Patter cake is getting to be an unbelievably boring game now I moaned, 'call an electrician' little voice said... 'OK, I think I will.' I replied back to the little voice.

I am now quite often talking to myself!

I never read the Blackrod News our local paper, I never usually buy one but the Saturday before whilst I was in the shop I purchased a newspaper. I had no idea why, I did not read it nor did I throw it away. Was this another sign I was receiving...

'Pass me the news paper' I said to my daughter 'I've had enough of this.' I turned to the page that advertises electricians and the very first one was a part p registered electrician, Result for me. I had listened and had bought the paper instinctively. I needed a part P electrician fast.

Well done the little voice said.

My daughter would not go out until she could have a quick dip in the bath and it was only ever a quick dip, even this was a tad touch and go with the old immersion tank that was my new hot water system, it worked sometimes but sometimes not and would only supply enough water for one to bath. It cost a fortune to boil, a ten foot kettle that rattled with disgust that we should even think about attempting to use it and would gush out brown water after she let you have five inches of clean water, telling us that was all she could manage. I am old and need to be replaced the old boiler stated. By now I had started to slack in the hygiene department. I did not care unless I was going to work or out and I hardly ever went out these days anyway. So we both sat and waited with no electric for the electrician to arrive and would you believe it as soon as the electrician walked through the door, it was like magic, Abracadabra the electrics came back on ... how bizarre how bizarre! 'Twenty pound call out charge please', the electric guy said to me. I handed him the cash, he looked at us like we were two deranged simpletons who clearly love nothing more than handing over cash for a call out fee for nothing.

I arranged for him to do a part P electrical safety test the following week.

The following week the electrical guy came as promised and carried out the part p electrical safety test. The electrics to the whole place failed big time. Unsatisfactory was what the report stated, Oh my, oh my. How it was very unsatisfactory the thieving fat little wanker I thought… Maybe I can now get out of this twelve month contract. My landlord had been reselling me electric at thirteen point five pence a unit then stealing it back off me, as switch four on the main consumers unit did not supply anything in my flat. Harry was running cable downstairs to the shop. He was using my pounds that the munch machine was chomping to supply himself with electricity. Well he who laughs last laughs longest I thought as I had been filling the munch machine with twenty pence coins.

I contacted the lovely lady from the council and informed her of the failed safety certificate and said I would email her a copy asap. The lady said by law I have to inform the landlord of the failed electricity test as these jobs were now considered priority. Harry was not allowed to rent the property out without a up to date certificate. I text Harry and take great delight in explaining that the part P safety test had failed miserably and as predicted, right on cue the electrics went off again.

Harry was at the squat quicker than the speed of sound, he marched straight over to the consumer unit and he played around with it, flicking switches off then on again. I was stood over him watching his every move, he flicked down the switch that was labeled number four and insisted that I should leave it off, and I wonder why that is I thought.

I had not emailed the certificate to him so he had no idea that I knew all about switch four. Harry then took out his keys and unlocked the meter, as he emptied the munch machine, his face went into some kind of deformed squashed appearance, like someone had just crushed his head right in front of me. He looked at me, then he looked again at the contents of the money holder and saw that instead of been filled to the brim with gold coloured pound coins. I had been feeding the money muncher with twenty pence coins. His head nearly blew right off his shoulders, if his head was a rocket and his body the launcher I reckon his head would have made it to

Jupiter. He was totally gobsmacked. 'This is a pound coin machine' Harry flipped out.

'Oh really' I replied 'It doesn't say insert one pound anywhere on the machine so I haven't broken any laws' I said feeling chuffed to bits with myself.

Harry was now flipping in such a rage he threw all the contents of the machine right back at me, twenty pence pieces littered all over the floor. He then stormed out shouting at me but completely forgetting to lock the meter.

As soon as Harry left I switched number four back on.

'What are you doing' my daughter asked 'Harry has told you to leave it switched off'

'Yes he would say that' I replied 'That how he has been stealing electric from me, if its running live downstairs let it shock him'.

A night or two later I could hear Harry working downstairs in the shop. I heard him scurrying about, like the rat that he was. I was delighted when I heard a little yelp, a crash of the ladders then silence... and my little voice said Harry has just had a electric shock'

'I know' I replied

The next morning I woke up to a text. Be out by Saturday or I will put the building up for sale.

'Who are you? My little voice said, Tommy Cooper The old magician. Move out Just like that!'

I laughed and replied 'no I am not' to my little voice, who had now developed a sense of humour.

Now the electrics were getting more erratic than ever. He would now start leaving the electric off for as long as he felt like it. It usually depended on what kind of mood he was in, so we played patter cake once again. I would text harry they would come back on. Late one Friday night my daughter tripped coming up the concrete steps, this time I went mental. The next day through a friend of a friend of a friend we managed to get hold of a generator.

I text Harry... I have had to buy a generator, I will deduct it from your rent. but I will not be paying you any more rent until all the jobs are sorted. I will put the money In a holding account. According to law if repairs need doing to a property and your landlord refuses to get the jobs done one is quite with in ones rights to with hold the rent.

I then went straight to Asda and bought a microwave. Ha I thought do what you like with the electrics. I was not as joyous when I realized that you cannot run a microwave off a generator but I am very pleased to say I have never had to use the generator. The electrics came back on and stayed on.

The sound of the generator would have had the neighbours complaining. Only once did I or was I able to fire up the worn out generator and man was it loud! It sounded like a worn out jumbo jet and it did not look much better, it was ancient. It was that old it could have been produced in five hundred BC but I managed to get it for free so I was not complaining, what a great big smelly thing that played the part, it fitted in perfectly in my unfinished kitchen.

I failed to notice the for sale sign that had been placed on to the squat when I was driving home from work the night before. I did not notice the sign until I looked out of the window Sunday morning. What a complete dick, he can do what he likes. Fuck him I thought and as I still had no lock on the pound muncher. I kept all the radiators on full day and night.

I was starting to feel unwell again 'what is wrong with me? I never have colds this much' I groaned. I was really poorly, my diet was poor, I was now living off microwave meals. I constantly felt sick whenever I did eat or drink.

I put the thought of me feeling rotten to the back of my mind and rang my daughter 'Harry has done it. He has put the building up for sale' 'what a prat' my daughter laughed. I was not laughing.

I was feeling too rotten to do anything, never mind moving all my stuff out again. But I now know I can get out of the twelve month contract.. I was struggling to move my body. So I went and laid down on the sofa, wondering where I was going to move to.

Thinking I would have the chore of house hunting again.

As I was lying there, just staring out of the window that afternoon. It was then when it happened. It was not like a bolt from the blue, I saw a males face, brown hair, blue eyes, he spoke to me. 'do I know you' his face looked familiar. I called him Grim

I had been experiencing some strangeness for quite a while seeing faces, the little voices in my head. I was thinking about the year before, the start, the finish what had happened, other people who I will refer to as big twats that I can not stand and if a massive steam train could run them all down one by one like they do in the cartoon road runner. I would be a happy chappy.

I was thinking about the squat I had come to live in and where I would like to live next. That normally I should feel a bit annoyed., angry, pissed off but I felt none of these emotions.

I felt weird; a very strange sensation like I had stepped out of my own body and someone else has jumped in.

I started to think about all the people who had caused me hurt and grief who threw poisoned darts when I was not looking. I started to think, they must have really sad pathetic life's to want to spend their energy bitching about me.

Forgive them...
'I will not'
Yes you will!
'No I will not'
I am taking to myself.
I am mad!

As I dissected each and every part of my life and I realized that forgiveness had been given without me even being aware that it had already been given,

This is totally without my consent.

The voices in my head were now doing a mini amount of squabbling.

Laying on the sofa staring out the window, seeing pictures in the clouds that made absolute no sense at all, I told myself this is it. You had better phone the hospital, book a room in the nut ward and put your name down for a bed... you have gone mad! No more nescafe for you... oh no caffeine free from now on.

I drifted off to sleep.

Two forty five am my phone started to ring, private number flashed on my caller ID. I answered the phone 'ello' was all I managed, as when you have been woken up in the early hours of the morning, you are not usually your chirpiest. 'Your fucking daughter' the voice said 'I'm gonna get her sorted, I will burn the flat down and kill you both, you will be raped'. At first I thought it was some mad mental person then it became clear it was a voice I thought I recognized.

I do not know what made me laugh., fear perhaps. I was shaking, what sick person rings in the midst of the night with such vile threats.

I was fuming, angry and scared. I then started pacing the squat up and down, up and down. I paced around none stop waiting for my daughter to arrive back home safe and sound from her weekend job as a barmaid.

I could not sleep, the phone call, the sickening early morning hour call, played on my mind like a record on repeat over and over again. I could hear his words, the conviction in his threats. I did not know what I should do.

Do I ignore the threat he has just told me I asked myself. No said the little voice you must send your child back to live with her dad.

The next day, I along with my family went out for a meal to celebrate my sisters birthday. I decided to tell all of the early hours phone call, we all decided whoever it was must have been drunk and at the same time agreed that my daughter was going to take a little holiday and move back with her dad.

I packed some personal things in a bag and kept them beside me. If he does set the place on fire at least I will have a few bits left I thought to myself.

During meditation I started to work on trying to balance my chakra, by now I was starting to hallucinate…who needs drugs when you can do chakra for free… same results.

I was still a bit sloppy when it came to grounding myself and would just float off anytime anywhere. I believe now is the time I should think about purchasing an indoor TV aerial, get a distraction, a cure!

Faces appeared- ghosts… who are you? I could not hear the faces talk this time, I could just see little faces. They say silence is golden, which shade of golden. Is it new crazy colour golden madness?

Book me that bed!

I decided the best way to see if I am really going crazy is to attend the spiritualist church so on a Thursday evening I set off to the church. Yes church is where I headed. We all sung in church. Abba, I believe in Angles… I felt a weird strangeness wash over me, just nerves I told myself. I was sat in the spiritualist church on my own, not that I felt stupid or out of place. I just had this weird strange vibe.

The medium stood on the main stage. Tonight's speaker was a middle age man who would be a channel for the dead spirits to pass on messages to their loved ones. I forget his name I will call him Bob, he was fantastic. I was amazed, wow so other people can hear voices and see the dead as well as me I thought.

A spirit came through, there was a young girl who was sat on the front row, with a couple of her school friends. The messages came through…. 'I am getting a message for someone, they want to tell you that the finished decorating in the hall looks nice, sorry I did not have time to finish it'… the young girl put her hand up as it was her father who had died of cancer. As she listening to Bob passing on her father's messages. I could tell she was in deep grief for her loss; the young girl laughed, cried, and understood everything Bob had told her.

After the service I decided to follow the regular group of church goers downstairs for a cup of tea and a biscuit.

I sat myself down on the same table as the frequent church goers. As I had a list of questions in my head that I was going to ask Bob or one of the other people that had got up in the closed circle who had communicated with the dead.

As I sat at a table with the other regular attendees not one person spoke to me…. where is the love that they preach I thought.

Bob was in conversation with a woman in ear shot of me… go on ask him the voice said. That is what you have come here for.

'Do you see pictures?' I blurted out at Bob.

'Yes I do' he replied. Bob could tell I was a little bit nervous and he came and sat next to me we chatted about what was going on in my head, another younger lady at the table spoke. 'What I cannot understand if it is me talking or them the dead talking to me'

"I am like that" I blurted out again.

Bob gave a lovely smile and said that you will be soon able to tell the difference as you will feel the different sensations.

Bob gave me a lot of advice, we chatted on things that have happened to me with the visions, plus the feelings I get when around certain people… Then a lovely Irish man sat at the table he asked me 'do you know how to shut off?'

'Shut off, no it is quite constant nowadays' I replied.

The Irish man told me that because I am able to communicate with spirit, (can I?!) And that being physic is different to communicating (erm is it?) but I also needed to be able to shut off. He said this was a very important thing to do every time you want communication to stop.

'I want it to stop permanently' I told him.

The Irish man just smiled and nodded his head and demonstrated how to shut off. 'You imagine the top of your head is wide open and you are closing down the shutter, then bolt it closed' he stood up to leave but said I should come back to go to church on Tuesdays and join their open circle.

'Were full' a woman snapped at me.

Steady on cow girl... chill out I wanted to tell her as that is just fine by me, as I am going home and shutting off.

Driving home I thought to myself... either I am not as mad as I think I am, or I have just been around a whole lot of folk who are as equally, no more mad than me.

TOTAL REWIND

Over the last few days, seems like weeks could even be months. I have no idea what day it is. Even stranger things are starting to happen in the squat the place feels much colder than ever before.

I head off out and go to my friends, I feel slightly uncomfortable, on edge, sitting around at my friends so I decided it was time for me to leave and to go back to the squat. I get in my car.

'What does this mean? Where am I going? 'I started the engine and I drove home. I could not understand there wasn't anything coming through. The radio was playing then suddenly the radio switched itself off. I sensed an edgy kind of calmness around me, a weird calmness. At home in the squat I turned on my laptop. I clicked for the internet and instead of welcome to three home page. I got:

"Error with server"

Code 536

Guru Meditation

In big black letters across the screen. 'What was going on?' I said feeling really panicked.

I turned round and there stood in the corner, was a ghost, maybe a guide, maybe a demon. A man I think I am not sure just a stiletto of the dark shadow, the whole seven months flashed in visions in front of my eyes. The night I got barred from my local. I was quite surprised as rumor had it that I was bouncing over the walls that I had been shouting and crying my eyes out, clinging to a bottle of red wine. When in fact I was sat outside the pub crying my eyes out over death, refusing to leave. Screaming at the sky.

Wow, I wasn't as bad as the back stabbers made out. Yep a little crazy but not that shocking that I will never be allowed to set foot in the place again. Plus I remember that night. As the night went on the visions got more intense. The flame of the candles flickered as if they were answering my questions, the flame rose higher for yes, in a circle for cannot tell just yet and side to side was no.

I was now communicating with a candle!

The days slipped into nights, the faces popping up everywhere, I was not sleeping, I was not eating, I constantly felt ill, whats wrong with me? I still hadn't gone to the doctors.

I called in sick that many time in the last past few months then I started to ignore request for hair to be done and I was letting clients down. I had just let my business slip away and now days and nights passed by, they just rolled over into one and still I had no sleep.

I had joined the living dead! I had started to hallucinate, a full on LSD trip. The faces became people, and the people had become real. They had moved in the living dead were everywhere. The smell of death, the stench was now in the air. I felt a tap from behind on my shoulder... 'Wake up call' a different voice sniggered. 'What do you want? Get the fuck out of my flat!' I screamed at them. What did they want with me?

They wanted me to follow them into the darkness, to the pits of hell. I was the leading lady of my very own horror movie. The darkness was now sucking on my soul. I could feel the heavy weight crushing my chest. I was struggling to breathe. I shouted out for my guides and my god.

'You have no god, you have not got a religion' they taunted me.

'I have got a god, I have got my God, I believe in my god' I screamed in their gray hollow faces.

'who is your God then?' the voice demanded...

The ghosts were trying to break me down. They were trying to bring me down. They followed me around, get out of my flat I demanded but they was not going anywhere, not without me, not tonight. They wanted to take me to the dark side...I prayed over and over.

May the angels keep you til morning.
May they guide you through the night.
May they comfort all your sorrows.
May they help you win the fight.
May they keep watch on your soul.
May they show you better ways.
May they guard you while you're sleeping.

May they see you through your days.
~ Author Unknown

The demons were trying to convince me that all is now theirs and that they had my soul.

I went into full hallucination.

I wanted my soul back but they had it. I felt empty inside, sunken. Where had my soul gone? My soul appeared in front of my face. 'You look like me but you are with the devil'. I said to my soul.

Had I sold my soul to the devil? I cannot remember doing that. I would not sell myself out, not to the devil. Would I? No way! My mind was now getting confused. I pleaded with my soul to come back to me but she refused, she was stuck in the dark place that she was in. Scared to be in the dark but too scared to let go.

'I do not want to be living in the dark' I demanded. 'Tell her that she, my soul better come back now' I told my guides... No was the answer. It was starting to became too much. Where did they all come from? Why are they here?

I was feeling jittery and on edge, overcome with anxiety and fear. I asked again for my soul back and still the answer was no. Have I sold my soul? I asked

'No way not in this lifetime' the little voice replied. I prayed that my soul would be rescued.

Madness. Crazy visions, I was being chased by dark spirits, by the ghosts. They had my soul and they also wanted me... 'I do not think so. I want my soul back' I said. I decided to go for a drive to clear my head, to get out of the squat to be away from the ghosts that were floating around me. I couldn't drive. I just sat in my car hallucinating, to scared to go back into the squat. After a few hours I plucked up the courage and I went back to my squat in the early hours of the next morning. The ghosts were now everywhere, sitting on my couch, floating on the stairs. Feeding from my fear like vultures on a carcass. I roamed around the squat. Visions appearing in the blank TV screen... You are not having me; I want my soul back its mine and I am having it back. I then prayed to my god to help me.

Paranoia was kicking in. The ghosts were now playing mind games they were filling my body with fear. I was being dragged into the darkness.

I could hear something banging around up stairs. I go to turn on my iPod to try and drown out the noises coming from above. The silence is now a shade of total madness. I switch on the iPod, save yourself by James Morrison was displayed, fear is overriding all logic 'not on this train' the little voice says. I can hear more banging; I am in a total state of terror, shadows flashing past my eyes.

I make my way up the stairs, I do not see anyone but I can sense the presence. I walk over to the attic cupboard convinced someone or something is hiding in there 'You don't want to sit downstairs being paranoid do you' said little voice. 'No' I replied. 'Lock them in the cupboard then' little voice encourages. I just stood there not knowing what to do.

'Go on, Lock them in if that is where they want to be, that is where they can stay' little voice repeats. I then stacked the unpacked boxes up against the attic cupboard door.

Did they get their kicks from placing me in fear? the ghost, the lost souls, the devil with his devil workers, was that what they needed to become stronger? Was it that they needed to take over my mind? 'They are too many of them to lock them all in' I cried..

I ran out of the squat and jumped into my car. I drove around looking for a church, for a priest to perform a exorcism. The ghosts had appeared in my car. 'Get out of my car' I screamed at them. They refused to leave. I drove to different churches but all the doors were locked. I finally found an open church, I had no idea what religion the church belonged to, I ran inside and found the man of his church. 'please' I begged 'bless my car, remove the dead'. My head was fried. The church man came to my car, he first helped me clean my car then he performed a blessing. He gave me a copy of the bible and told me to read and pray. Not long after the man of his church had blessed my car the ghosts had gone... they had vanished. Had the church man removed the ghosts?

But shortly afterwards they reappeared again like crack addicts who needed a fix. Only this fix was from my fear and the addiction was me.

Devil workers, the soul sucking vampires had started to reappear in the back seat of my car. What the fuck! I drove to the all night supermarket and bought a load of garlic. I started unpeeling the garlic and ate the garlic. I then filled my car with the garlic and hung them like a cross from my dashboard mirror. 'Eat more garlic then' little voice said. ' Eat it quick' the voice sounded urgent. What the fuck is going on? I ate huge cloves of garlic.

What was it they had a planned? I was trying not to drown. I was being sucked deeper into the underworld. I drove from Blackrod to the next town Landswood back to Blackrod back to Landswood, back and forth to- and- fro. 'I need to go to the monastery' I yelled at the voice.

'Do not make me a nun!' The little voice screamed. 'If I cannot go to the monastery then I need a church' I answered back. But as I approached the churches the doors then closed. I needed somewhere safe. Where could I go? Had I let these negative spirits in? Had I allowed them into my world and they were now sucking on my soul?

I had not sold my soul. I was standing firmly with my faith, with my god. They had stolen my soul. They had tricked me into handing my soul over in my dark despair. I had not protected myself enough or properly. I needed help. I had let them feed and grow off my fear. My phone had no battery life left. I got out my car and just left it. I was hallucinating again, another full blown trip. I started running with the ghost chasing me. I went to a friend house and stayed with her.. My head was ready to snap, the faces the voices-the melt down.

Confessions of love, Lust at first sight
A bird of prey with passion you fly
Never any gray bits, It's black or it's white
Swooping down like a vulture
With a charming raptor
Captivated in the grasp of your claws
Powerful manipulation, Piercing the flesh
Possession Rebellion Domination
Now you are saying you want to be free?
Gliding you fly almost effortlessly
A thousand meters you spot you're pray
The salvage, the hunter, the old world vulture
Style sophistication the hunger the greed
Soaring the sky for the ultimate feed
Creatures of darkness floats in the air
Underestimated misunderstood
Claiming their victim drinking their blood.

DEATH

I am living alone. Just me my thoughts and them!
The dead!

The loss of a loved one is a very painful time, grief, guilt, could, would, should are emotions that can over ride all logic. All things have been shaken all over the place. Take a beautiful hand crafted three storey dolls house, with all the miniature furniture neatly placed where it should be and along comes someone and picks up the house and chucks it down the road, shaking all the contents up and down round and round.

Put me down the house demands...

'OK'

Smash.

Leaving mini furniture out of place and broken.

'Do not let this affect the kids' my voice used to tell me. 'Put it away until a later date'.

So I put a smile on my face and carry on with the pretend happy life. I have been wearing an all weather survival kit, a water proof plaster cast on my heart. The plaster cast has now come loose, no longer does it want to stay on but I am not ready yet. I am not ready to deal with the pain, the emotions. 'Get back on' I scream at the cast – I have got no chance the cast is cracking... it is starting to slip off.

'You are going to face this' the little voice is saying.

'I don't want to deal with it. I am not ready' I plead.

I crack on, trying to keep everything wrapped up inside. Carry on with the show... Then Boom

Emotions are out: I scream 'Why - what happened?

Panic and despair kick in and with it comes losing pride. Going for days without really washing, I mean I splashed my face, half heartily with water, brushed my teeth, put a different hat on to hide the unwashed, unkept hair, still wearing the same clothes that I have slept in for the past four of five nights. They are doing the job of keeping me warm. It does not matter any way I do not care. I am now down in the pit hanging with the dead, who are sucking on my soul, crazy thoughts popping into my head.

Rational behaviour has left the station next train is going to darkness. What/ why/ where? I do not want to go into the darkness. But I am on the train, on the journey sinking, sliding further down the snaky slippery slope.

Unable to control the thoughts; I want to flick them off. Where is the switch? The deep rooted fears that is now eating away at my soul...

'Help me then' I demand to my guides, the angles, god and goddess, the spider on the wall, anyone who will listen. Placing blames on people around, sinking further and further down asking myself, is there a bottom?

Clutching all I can, frantically trying to cling to the edges in a desperate attempt to climb back up. When will I finally stop sinking?

Then the Angles arrive lifting me up, helping me get my foot back on the ladder. One step at a time they encourage and once again I start to feel safe. Wrapped up in the love that is trying to surround me.

Not on this train ride baby, this journey is going down to the bottom and before I know it I can feel myself getting sucked back down, pulled in to the darkness. The voices are getting louder errantly chattering inside my head. 'So you think you're in control?'

I am now living with the dead. The ghosts are floating around. Their faintly faces popping up, they form and appear like shadows. Confused to what is or who they are... is this real?

Am I mad?

Who is my spirit guide, my main man and who is my guru? Who are the ghosts? What do they want?

I am struggling to cope. I want it to stop. I am really trying my best to try and stop it to switch it off. I shout out 'I want it stop, turn it off, change the station, change the channel' but however hard I try I cannot get it to turn off. Why won't it turn off? I scream.

My eyes are wide open like an owls, the Full moon is approaching. I decide it would be best to stay in for a few days. I tell myself over and over that I must stay in DO NOT GO OUT! I feel tense, slightly jittery and borderline on edge. I try to avoid the darkness that is pulling me in towards it. I sit in silence praying that the phase of the moon won't entice me into the dark.

Faces of ghost popping up everywhere. The voices that fill me with self doubt and fear are slowly clawing in to my thoughts, making their way into my mind. Am I being watched? I have a feeling that I am not alone.

Visions popping into my mind. Elephants are carrying people on their backs into the big sea of mud. The mud is rising higher and higher the elephants disappear under the mud, where have they gone?

People's bodies are sinking into the mud until slowly the whole body is covered in mud. Fast forward people are covered in mud and they are fighting in the dark, the battle field far away in the distance.

I start to pray, I am going mad! 'I don't care -start praying now!' The voice demands.

I pray and I pray over and over.

'God help me' - and god helps me, sending his A team down to comfort me, whispering reassurance, calm down now come on take deep breaths. You know the drill. Again you try to climb the ladder. You are getting closer... Nope something happens.

Visions are getting more vivid. Little people are rolling a massive rock up a hill, I squint, I can barely see the TV that is my mind. They are trying to push the rock with all their strength, struggling to get the rock up the hill. Fast forward I am standing on a cliff ledge, nowhere to go just standing there too scared to jump off and too scared to go back. Rewind I am lost in the forest that has over grown with trees, roots coming out of the ground trying to entangle me in there grasp that wants to take me to the underworld. Fast forward again I am by the ocean the sea breeze flowing freely through my hair.

Pulled back and forth making no sense; I try to work it out. What is going on? I feel like I am being pulled from darkness to light: Pulled backwards then forwards then back again. I pray. I want to be in the light. I close my eyes praying to Angles, to God, to my guides to guide me.

Angel Michael shine down on me

Send a pillar of light to me

Help me here and now

Save me from physic attack.

Pulled back and forth darkness to light over and over again. I pray that the full moon would pass.

Go away; I don't want to hang out with the dead, the living dead all existing in the dark. The state of confusion in the atmosphere when hanging out with the dead is sucking away my soul. I am sliding back down to the very pit of the black hole. My mind starts to play its very own arcade game; self doubt vs. free will. Two sides battling in the dark, self doubt is in the lead.

I am now starting to feel lifeless. Depression is kicking in. Nervous breakdown is second left just past the traffic lights. I am trying to fight but they are surrounding me, closing in. Crushing me, I am screaming, shouting, pleading and begging for help...

PRAY PRAY PRAY

Then calmness overrides. Self doubt is backing away. Angels and guides come rushing in to the rescue like missionaries with blankets, layers of blankets LOVE FAITH HOPE they wrap them around my body lifting and rocking my soul gently like a new born child. A magnetic force giving me energy to help my soul, lifting it out of darkness, lending me a torch as I roam around in the dark unable to see the light, fighting my way through the forest of over grown trees rooted deep into the core.

Days were becoming nights that just rolled over back in to the day. I run to church, faces everywhere, in pictures, just appearing... GET OUT OF MY HEAD. They had followed me here. Do they not realize where I am, where I have walked into? I sit down on the bench, I see the faces appear before my eyes in the old wooden church floor...This is real, my mind pops. In my utter desperation I started to panic and grab people bibles out of their hands and started dropping the bibles on to the faces of demons. The soul suckers - faces appearing in the floor boards. I chucked one bible on each head.

The Priest, Bishop or minister I'm not sure what religion of church it was that I had just ran in. The man of his church stopped what he had intended to say to the congregation, his planned out speech, and looked at me and said a prayer.

'Dear lord, let us pray for this child'

The soul sucking devil workers suddenly started flying out of the window, like faint shadows of tiny bats, making screaming sounds,

What have I done?

I have just walked in to Gods house picked up a load of god's books and chucked them on his floor.

Great move, now what am I supposed to do, I was trying to think, all the other church goers staring at me.

'DID YOU SEE THEM LEAVE'? I ask the lady next to me.

'Have they all gone'? Everyone looked at me in silence; the church was silent with a chill that ran down my spine, through the air.

I left church, shit I thought I still hadn't been blessed I still haven't been christen by the man of his church.

Why didn't I get christened?

'Because I do not want to be that religion' my voice screamed. 'Stay with your faith'.

My stomach began to make loud rumbling noises, weird peculiar noises that were getting louder and louder. I can now feel a sensation of something crawling under my skin.

They are trying to get inside my body - they want to take over my mind!

I run out of church and down the road in to a betting shop, where small groups of men are hanging out, waiting for the next scheduled horse race. All eyes watching the big screen TV's hoping that today would finally be there lucky day and they would get a win on the bets they had placed.

I run into the toilet and slam the door behind me.

I sit on the floor and I pray. A vision of my soul appears on the back of the door.

My soul looks sad, lonely, lost, hurt and in pain.

'I want my soul back' I cried to the door 'you are not having me'.

'you sold me out to the devil' my soul replied.

Had my soul now become a creature of the night, trapped in the darkness?

I prayed to god, to the creator, to the main man, to the angles, the Sun, the Moon, Earth to come and help me rescue my soul.

'Please help me' I cried, begged and I pleaded.

I tried to grab my soul: but you have sold me was all that I heard; the fight began with me and the angles at one side, the devil the other.

Things started to get worse, each time the angles were fighting to rescue my soul back, the devil workers were pulling me back in.

I could feel the pain in my stomach; they were trying to detach my soul from my body. I was being pulled from one side to the other, both the angles and the devil grabbing at me, both pulling at me. I am heaped on the floor 'go home' the angles whispered 'we have a better chance there'.

I left the betting shop and headed around the corner to collect my car where I had abandoned it a few nights before. I saw a dark figure sat on the back seat.

'There are more of them' I screamed to my guide. I started to run, but run where?

Where am I going? Go to church the voice was shouting in my head, run now get to church.

The next nearest church was only a few minutes away. I sprinted around the corner. I was running faster than I have ever ran before. 'There she is' I heard one of them shout, 'get her'. The dark figures were all over. I was just about to put my foot over and step into the church garden, when I felt someone push me. I went down, slam onto the concrete floor. I felt the sensation of my throat being sliced. Blood was dripping from my mouth they had sliced my throat from the inside. They are trying to cut my throat.

I tried to get up, my head felt dizzy. I had completely lost my orientation. I manage to stumble into the church. I sit on the bench and I pray.. I see vision of the battle that's going on to claim my soul. I tried to grab my soul.

The church I was now in was like ice. Get her out, one of the church goers said to the priest. We cannot evict this child from gods house said the priest. All the church goers got up and left.

This is not a house filled with love I thought, the visions re appeared, vividly in my mind. Angles verses devil in the fight for who would claim my soul.

An ambulance arrived and with the blood coming from my mouth I was taken to hospital. The devil worker also got in the ambulance with me. I sat in silence as the sirens echoed throughout the vehicle.

I was then taken by the paramedic into a small room, A nurse came in the room and asked me my name, I told the nurse my name. The nurse then looked at my mouth and my throat, after she had checked me out she then gave me something to gargle. I was then told to wait whilst she went for a doctor, not a chance I thought. I am getting out of here!

The visions were intense. 'Cut her throat, get her raped' the shadows were saying, chanting, they the ghosts were now all around me, visions flashing in front of me.

My soul was wrapped up in cloth and petrol was doused over me. I - My soul was dragged, and then hung from a stake. A wooden cross. Wood piling high all around touching my feet, The wood was then set on fire. The flames of the fire rising. People were dancing around me, throwing more petrol over me, keeping the fire alive. My soul was being burnt. I put my hood up and prayed to angel Michael, to my guides, to God to please came and put out the burning fire.

The sky above then poured rain over the fire, but I was dead!

The soul suckers were everywhere I turned, they were all over the hospital. I have got to get out of here. I have got to go right now. I ran out of hospital. I had to get home to rescue my soul. I went for taxi and set off again to collect my car. One of the devils workers appeared in the taxi. 'Each time you try and get your soul back we will slice your throat a little bit more' the devil worker warned me.' You will feel the pain from the inside out, you must join us tonight, commit suicide and join us'.

I got out the taxi. The dark shadows still waiting for me in my car. I started to panic my throat was sore.

'I don't want to die' I begged my God

There are in my car again! I silently cried to My Guides. 'You have got to get home' my guide said so we can get your soul back. You just need to get home'.

I shouted at the devil workers to get out of my car and screamed at the ghosts to leave me alone.

As I went to put my key in the door of my car a police officer came over he was rude, he was one of them, a devil worker, one who had given their soul to work for the devil. There were workers everywhere. The devil worker started asking me questions I was confused and I was asked to do a breathalyze test.

'I have not even got in my car yet how can I be drink- driving' I screamed at this devil worker. I haven;t been drinking. I am now arguing with the ghosts and the devil workers. The voices in my head telling me I've got to go home. I then slap the devil worker across the face. Cuff her he said to his college.

I struggled with the devil worker dressed as a policeman. 'Get off me' I yelled 'I need to get home'. 'I need to go home to get my soul back from your boss the devil' I was thrown in the back of the police riot van. The devil worker was also in the back of the van. I then managed to remove one hand from the cuffs with the help of the angles and keep the devil worker away from me. Fighting, arguing in the back of the police riot van. His dark face, the big hooked nose and his dark black eyes sent shivers that were running down my spine. 'were going to rape you Maggie' they hissed.

I was dragged from the van into the station then to the duty desk. The police who was one of them was insistent that I had been drinking. 'Breathalyse me' I screamed. I was asked to hand over my possessions. An itinerary was written. I was then taken to the cell. The door was locked.

I felt a chill in the air. I was alone in a cell, surrounded by death, trapped and nowhere to go. There was a red light coming from the camera in the ceiling. I stood there and prayed to the angles for protection. Shouting, screaming, begging for protection. I did not want to die. I do not want my soul to be destroyed or to be spiritually raped by evil spirits working for the devil, not in a cell, not anywhere.

I begged angel Michael to protect me to help me win the fight to gain back my soul... angles appeared at the tiny windows offering light and protection. Angel Michael came with two other angles into my cell, we prayed, the demons started coming in through the walls. I stood and fought against the demons.

I was amazed at the mist that started coming out through my finger, that formed a seal to prevent them fully forming and merging through the walls. They, the ghosts came in all forms but I was safe with the Angles protection that had been sent from God to help me. The workers were now stuck in the ground and in the walls or where ever they had tried to get in. Pieces of devil workers were splattered around my cell.

I was tired and I wanted to be released. I banged on the door 'let me out now' I begged the police. Nobody came. I felt slight relief as the soul sucking demons were now unable to get in and the ones that had got in had been demolished. I felt a sense of serene. I had won, there were none left to fight. The atmosphere seemed calmed the red light on the camera had been switched off. I sat and thought I would try to get some sleep.

I was woken up by the police devil worker opening the cell door window…' We will be back again later'. The police devil worker told me… Fear again crept all over me. I sat and prayed but all I could hear was a low whizzing noise. I started feeling uneasy. A feeling that something was wrong, something was defiantly wrong. I banged on the door 'I have got to get out, I have got to get home' I screamed. I turned around, the little square windows at the back of the cell had orange eyes peering in. I was surrounded by evil. The angles would not be able to hear my cries. The devil workers have lowered the frequency. I prayed to God over and over. If the Angles cannot hear me now please protect me, please make sure I come through this alive, whatever happens I do not want to live it. But keep me alive.

I prayed to the Sun, to my God.

I prayed and hoped and kept my faith. As the devil worker started to reappear I carried on fighting, smashing the demons, the ghost with the thin blue mattress, as the demons tried to jump onto me, ghost all around me. I am screaming to the Sun and the Moon until finally I feel like I have been drugged. I can barely stand. I sit on the cold stone concrete bed. Crazy thought take over my mind. I don't want to die I cry…

I wake up.

I am alive. Parts of the workers are now in bits and pieces stuck to my cell floor. Had God heard my pleas and sent the Angles back. - I am cold. I am not allowed a blanket.. I get up to get the stinky blue mattress from the other side of the cell and place it back on the concrete bed. I sit on the concrete bed with the mattress now back on it. I look down at the cell floor, the floor is sticky with the mist that was used to stop the devil workers from spiritually raping me. I hear a voice, I look down and see a figure, a face, it appears to be a male of some kind but he is not human. lying next to him is what seemed to look like a female, going nearer to the door there were two more flattened bodies who appeared to be older teenage girls/young women lying opposite sides to each other and then another one against the door, he looked male. I spoke to the man next to me. I told him I wanted my soul back. It was my soul they had no right keeping it. The two teenage girls were unable to budge as the stuff the Angles had sprayed was preventing them from moving. The woman spoke, she said I had stamped on her daughters face in church, and now this is what she would look like forever.

I was now wanted by the underworld.

I went in to shock.

My head was filled with fear, everything that had happened since the ominous early morning call had me terrified, terrified with fear that over the weeks built up in my head, lack of sleep was filling my mind with crazy thoughts, no wonder some use this method to torture people, lack of sleep can turn the healthiest of minds into pure despair – panic –detachment from logic- All bets are off, next train coming in is to crackdown!

My mind was now playing tricks, irrational thoughts brought on paranoia, my brain scrambling to receive information, mixed wiring, fuses blown, call that little man in your brain –the wires need fixing! The wires are now starting to melt-melting into each other. Confusion, misjudgment, fear, anxiety, momentarily loss of reality, the little part of the brain under the hustle and bustle of the flames of smoke, smoldering from all the melting wires. The voice in your head is screaming GET SOME SLEEP... SLEEP.

How can I sleep I shout back, I can see the atmosphere in the air like little particles floating around, each bumping into each other. I can see them, the dead all around me, did they follow me here? Have I really gone mad? Has my mind popped? Or is this real? Mental Mickey with a ticking clock... ticktock ticktock one o'clock, ticktock ticktock two o'clock ticktock ticktock three o'clock and time goes on and on.

I had felt it coming, the pulling the pushing the anxiety, the confusion in my mind. Only to wake up, I don't remember going to sleep- I am alive! Mixed emotions I am at the bottom of the pit, degraded, deranged, disgusted. I've spent the night screaming, fighting GET OUT OF MY HEAD. I've lost the plot, but I am alive. RELIEVED.

It is now daylight again.

I need the toilet. I bang on the cell door shouting that I need to go to the toilet. Eventually when I thought I was going to have to urinate on the floor, a police woman opens the cell door window. 'I need the toilet' I tell the police woman. She just nods her head, closes the hatch and unlocks the door.

I follow the police woman down the corridor to the toilet. I see cats all along the corridor, blurry faces on the wall.

There isn't a door on the toilet, just a inadequate piece of cloth, to small for the opening, pathetically hanging. The toilet stinks. A stainless steal toilet with no toilet seat, I try to adjust the curtain for some privacy, the police woman just stares at me. I hover over the rim of the seat so my skin doesn't touch the stinking toilet. I urinate. The cats have followed me into this tiny cubicle and jump onto my body, trying to scratch at my eyes. I start shouting for the cats to leave me alone.

'I want to go home' I tell the police woman. 'when can I go home' the police woman ignores me. I am then taken back to the cell.

Minutes feel like hours.. time ticks on…

The cell door then opens, two riot police ask me to follow them…

An eventful weekend. I had tried to go to church and was taken to hospital, I am arrested again and spend another night in the cells.

I am then taken by the police to hospital.

MENTAL INSTITUTION

So I am here at the Mental hospital.
I am accompanied by two riot officers, they hold my belongings, one standing either side of me. I'm having more hallucinations, I hear voices shouting in my head. I'm in a daze waiting to see a doctor.

I can see God fighting the Devil.., two shadows across the hallway.

I see a face on the wall. Then a ghost appears, the same guy from before, brown hair and blue eyes.. he tells me he is with me, by my side. I'm anxious, on edge. I ask if I can go for a cigarette. The policeman says no, I plead, he agrees. We, the two police officers and myself, stand outside the main entrance of the mental hospital. I am stood with my back against the wall, the two police are standing in front of me, so I don't run off. I finish my cigarette and am then taken to a small room.

I am in a nut house, a mental institution.

We wait for hours.

The doctor finally arrives he asks me question after question, I lie. I need to go home, back to the flat, to save my soul. The doctor then speaks to one of the police officers outside of the room. I cannot hear what is being said.

I am placed on a section.

The two riot police then escort me through the building into another part of the hospital.

We walk down a long corridor to a reception area.

The police officer speaks to the receptionist. The receptionist then picks up the phone and informs the ward that I have arrived.

A nurse opens the security doors.

As soon as I step through the security doors I silently pray..

Get me out of here!

I am shown to the dorm and to my bed by the nurse, which was now my new bedroom for the next foreseeable future. Placed on a section, I cannot leave. I am to share this room with five other women. I sit on my bed and pray to my God and my spirit guide, to come and guide me, to help me, to get me out of here. It's full of mental patients.

I pray to my guides, my God to save my soul.

I am now a mental patient.!

Had I allowed the demons to feed on my soul? My fear?

Am I mad?

I am taken to see another doctor. The psychiatrist, Question after question he asks me.. I tell the truth.

'Are you taking any drugs?

'No' I reply..

'Were you drinking alcohol?

'No' I reply..

'Have you been sleeping?'

'No' I replied 'I can't sleep'

Have you been hearing voices?

'Yes' I say

'Who does the voice sound like? The doctor asks

'Is the voice male or female?'

I try to tell the psychiatrist that they are ghost, they are real and I need to get home to reclaim my soul.

'Do the voices tell you to harm yourself Maggie?' the doctors asks

'Have you tried to harm yourself'

'What? You think I am on drugs and I want to harm myself? I didn't want to answer anymore questions. Doctors only work on logic and I couldn't understand the doctors logic, they don't listen. 'We will just take a few blood samples and send them off for testing' - A nurse then takes blood from my vein. - 'in the mean time' the psychiatrist carries on - 'we will give you some medication to stop the voices and something to help you sleep'

'Oh no! No way… I don't want medication I want spiritual healing, leave me alone' and with that I got up and stormed off out of his office and go back to my dorm.

My spirit guide has now come to my rescue. I can see the light workers, the angels… up and down in the tunnel of of darkness, trying to reach the light .. I start pacing around placing protection around my bed. Talking, crying, laughing with my most highest guides.

I did not have to ask the other women in the dorm if it would be OK for them to leave, they disappeared. I need to save my soul. The other patience are a bit shell shocked at the new patient, me. As I set about reclaiming my soul. Fighting the devil and the demons, Shouting 'if I am going down, if I'm going to hell to be claimed by the underworld, we are all going down'. I marched around the dorm demanding and commanding Divine Light, the Sun, the Moon and Earth.

I was now calling out to both Jesus and Satan.

Who is my God? Which angle is who? Is Jesus really real? Does Satan exist? Is Lucifer the devil? Old Lore - was the Devil really a Angel once before? Is there a heaven? Is there a hell? I throw a penny down a wishing well and pray to the Sun and the Moon. To Mother Nature, to Mother Earth. I fight the demons, I place a curse upon them. I cast a spell, I make a wish, I pray for a better tomorrow starting today - Set me free, free my mind. Bring me good blessing and all I deserve, as I stand here in the universe. Lead my into divinity, into sublime. For ghosts are real, their spirit is alive. For my imaginary friend is by my side. I call him Grim, I knew him in life, he says he's alive. I needed confirmation. Your not alive - you are dead. Why are you in my head? We argue, we laugh, we talk. I see his face, I see his smile, I love his style - I hear his voice definitely male - heaven sent to me. Or maybe I have been sent to him. Living in the astral world of temporary insanity, whilst I stand here with Grim in my mixed up reality on planet Earth.

Sixth-sense we shall see, if we make it to eternity. And what if we do? Who is my God?

I carried on with the battle with the devil and the demons that were dragging me, my soul around the dirty streets of the underworld, I was trying to reclaim my soul, spinning into the dark, frantically trying to reach the light at the end of the tunnel...Lost in my mind, the crazy mentality of what is reality, the isolation, the fear, the night mares, the flash backs. How can it be real. My mind is racing, I am stood naked in a field.

I had gone to bed, where had I been? A crazy nightmare, the violation inside. Where are my children. I had no time to cry. Where am I? how do I get back? I screamed at the sky, the night was black. Where have you been?

My children asked as they opened the door. My heart was pounding, as I looked at their sleepy faces a thousand miles from home. I shut the door and dressed in a hurry, as I muttered I must have been sleep walking, your both OK, try not to worry. I buried it with a smile and locked it in my head. I slipped in to the darkness, into my very own hell. I was now unworthy, lost all ego, gave away my pride as well. Emotionally destroyed I was hurting inside.

I put on a brave face, I kept my self going, time kept rolling. I pushed down the demons but they kept reappearing. I couldn't make it stop till finally my head went pop. I couldn't take anymore, I need change. I want change. I prayed to my God, to heal my mind, my body and my soul. Release me from this prison my life has become. I kept my faith. I talked to the Moon, as I sat in the room of the mental institution. Wondering if this is all real or just an illusion. Dazed at the past year and all the confusion, of what has gone on.

Lonely, depressed. Had the demons won? The voices in my head. The fear deep inside. I ask over and over, was it my fault? What happened? is this real? The pain, the nightmares, the delusional year that followed. I prayed to the angel, I prayed to my God to take away my misery and fill my heart with love. To take away the anger, the bitterness and pain. I asked God- would I feel safe again? Never again would I be frozen in fear. Release me from the nightmares that have consumed me for years. To take away the flash backs, help me stop the tears that I shed. Remove the demons from my head. To stop the visions that are destroying my mind. I hysterically cried.

I reached the light and jump in. I had saved my soul. I then set about cleansing my soul, freeing my body from the soul suckers that had attached themselves to me. My loving spirit guide guided me into spiritual cleansing that consisted of quite a lot of Tai Chi. At the time it seemed to have lasted for hours and hours, maybe it did. I have no concept of time. This is one of the most amazing spiritual healing feeling I have ever received. I will never ever in my life receive or feel what I felt right then, no words would be good enough to describe this amazing feeling. Never again in my life will I feel so much tranquility and inner peace. Divine light!

Was that real?

After removing of these negative energies, evil spirits and devil workers,

I wondered if they would now have to pray to my God to have mercy on their souls. for the invasion, violation and the takeover of another soul.

To complete my spiritual cleansing, my loving guide danced away with me in the shower, I could hear music playing. My guide showing me how to cleanse from the top of my head to the tips of my toes, so I could remove the black shadow and to revive my soul. The shadow then slowly started changing from black to white. It was a beautiful experience.

It is real!

But until the results from my blood test came back I am now sectioned under section twenty eight of the mental health act, that means for this month I will be living hospital life.

I phone my sister.

The rules of the hospital are: you are not allowed a belt or a razor, nail clippers or nail varnish remover, pens or pencils, boiled sweets or lighters. all these items have to be kept in a locked draw and you must have permission from a member of staff if you require to use one of these items. If a staff member thinks you are in a stable enough state, you can shaves your legs or armpits then hand them back in when finished and must never be given to another patient ever.

'Am I allowed out?' I ask

'No dear, you have been sectioned you can now only go around the hospital ward'.

My sisters are allowed to visit me. My sister brings me some pajamas, toiletries and some cigarettes. I love my sister. I give my sister my car keys so she can collect my car for me.

There is a washing machine on the ward, I wash my dirty clothes. I have another shower and put on the clean pajamas. The patients, all get to go for cigarette breaks during the day. like cattle being shifted from one cage to another, every few hours for ten minutes at a time.

This can become a way of life, some women have become institutionalized and they have friends in here.

Night 2

The food is not that bad. Or is it just I have been really ill and my diet has been poor.

I feel strange living the life of mental patient. Am I mental? Am I mad? Why can I see the dead and you cannot?

It is not for me being in here I tell my guides, I am not keen on this dorm sharing; the atmosphere is a bit edgy.

A young girl, she must only be in her late teens early twenties, has tried to cut her face off like it was a mask with a broken throat lozenge. That shit is not normal, something is bothering that kid; to want to remove her own face. I would never have thought that a boiled sweet could do so much damage. Would that young girl not be better having regression therapy to find the origins of emotions? Sometimes psychomatic physical problem can go back from experiences in a past life or childhood.

Have I been reborn?

Do we experience death and rebirth - some say we do, some say we don't.

Have I been suppressing emotions, that were brought to the surface, with the ominous early hours of the morning threatening phone call, to set me on fire and have me raped? I had never really thought about what happened abroad. I went sleep walking. Last thing I remember is I went to bed. I had put it in the cardboard box! Thank God both my children were alright.

What did happened? How did I end up sleep walking, to wake up naked? I will never know. I have no memory, the memory has never come back. I only have nightmares and flashbacks. But is it real? Then I thank my God again as my children were safe, they came to no harm. Mum just went sleepwalking!

Another younger girl, the youngest on the ward, has stuck a sharpened pencil in her bottom. That must of hurt like hell, she cannot walk, she is in pain, she then inflicts herself with more pain, then she is told by the staff if she wants to go with the rest of us for a cigarette break she has to walk. Her body is covered in big scars, she was picked on, bullied at school. She hides from life behind the walls of the hospital..

How much pain is this young girl in, spiritually, emotionally and mentally to do that? It doesn't seem right. I struggle to get my head around it.

One woman escaped at breakfast how she got out and got past the security doors and the walls surrounding the building, I have no idea. I would have left with her if I had known the escape route. Another patient has just kicked off with staff members, security rush in forcing the woman down, she is screaming, something is going on in her head, she is struggling to cope, she is then taken to the other side of the ward and placed in a single padded cell.

The woman opposite me before my arrival slashed her arms to bits. Which are now all stitched up, she is now been stabbing her stitched up arm with a pen. She has been doing this in private.

Why would she do that? I ask. The tip end of the pen has snapped in her arm with the blue ink leaking. The doctors are unable to remove the tip end from her already infected arm, she cries throughout the night from the pain. She will have to have her arm amputated.

Some of the woman on this ward are highly disturbed and dosed up on drugs, medication for treatment. Does this numb the pain? Making people become comfortably numb? Will I soon also become comfortably numb.

Night 3

Another terrible night's sleep. I have decided I am going to have to beg for a strong sleeping tablet. I realize now that I have chopped my nose off to spite my face when I refused any of the sleeping tablets.

'I have not come in here a drug addict, I am not leaving as one' I snapped at the doctor. I go and ask for a sleeping tablet.

The woman who has the bed next to me, the escapee, has been brought back by the police, she has been drinking a concoction of super tenants with vodka shots, she was violently sick throughout the night choking on her own vomit at one point, it was disgusting. I got out of bed and sat with her whilst she puked all over, I was trying to help her by getting her water and rubbing her back.

I now feel mentally and physically exhausted. And I also feel saddened.

There is a gym in the ward with nothing else happening in my day. I ask if I can use it. I ask my daughter to bring some gym clothes for my gym induction the following day. There is nothing to do stuck in here that in itself is enough to drive a person crazy.

My beloved daughter brings me a pair of her dads old Nike tracksuit bottoms, a bottle of diluted orange juice and a packet of family size of quavers and some more cigarettes. That's the annoying thing about getting sectioned they don't let you nip home to pack a bag and I didn't pack a bag in advance just in case I ever got sectioned.

Woman are getting agitated waiting for Ten pm to arrive so they can queue for pain killers or medication. Women are crying to go home or because they want extra pain killers, I feel comfort knowing my spirit guide and my imaginary friend are with me. I can sense their presence.

Night 4

I had a reasonably good night sleep last night. I also went to the gym session this morning, I'm in bad shape. All the other women were in the TV room so I was able to spend a good hour alone in the dorm meditating and doing Tai Chi afterwards.

I saw a male, a African he had short dreads in his hair, he was wearing a white tee shirt with plain green combat pants and trainers. He just stood there, standing next to the bed opposite. I felt safe in his presence. I thought he was Angel Michael.

I managed to grab a few hours sleep this afternoon, which is a good thing. I also spoke to the woman in the bed next to me who had escaped, her arms show very large scars from self harming, I ask her why she would want to cut herself and what she said is really sad.

Her story is her son, her first born died just before his eighteenth birthday, her husband then died three months later, she replied; 'Because it's the only pain I can control' She is unable to let go of the pain of losing her child and her husband, because if she did she would feel like she was letting go of them.

Have I been holding on to my pain? Pain from broken hearts, betrayal and death, suppressed emotions and fear?

Am I lucky that I was able to release it let it go?

I have been given unescorted freedom today which means I can go to the canteen without a member of staff and also use the computer room, for one hour per day, at set times. What a lucky mental patient I feel!

I am still waiting for the results of my blood test.

Night 5

Yet another terrible night of trying to sleep, it's loud at night on the ward, pitching a tent on the M1 would be a vast improvement in noise reduction.

I am feeling tired and energyless. I Feel like shit.

This is real. I'm in a mental hospital!

I almost sure, no I am 100% positive my own efforts for spiritual cleansing with the guidance of my spirit guide have removed the dark spirits that were clinging to my soul. I am starting to feel weary, a bit creeped out being in a place like this, where if women have not self harming they are trying to commit suicide.

Being in here is getting me down I am starting to get even more depressed.

I was depressed before I came in, I feel like a few more weeks in here I might be diagnosed with severe depression. I have got to get out.

'What you doing when you do that weird stuff?' one of the women asked me.

'I am meditating and cleansing my soul' I replied.

She tells me I am mad.

I feel real empathy for the women who came and sat on my bed and told me their story. The pain that weighs on their soul, on their mind.

Thinking do we woman in the nut house get offered alternate therapy, spiritual healing, some Reiki Healing, have light yoga and breathing classes to help the chakra system to free and remove blockages.

This is ancient theory it has worked for thousands of years. Spiritual healing is the way to go..

Doctors who want to carry on numbing the pain with a combination of medications.

Why don't they want to help find the trigger to our pain to get deep to the core to find the way to release?

I do not want to spend my life fucked up on prescribed drugs. If I was going to take drugs, I would smoke or use something produced naturally on Gods Earth. Maybe more natural remedies are required, go back to the way the ancient practiced.

I do not want to be munching anti depressants, anti psychotic or other medicine produced by the mass.

Become A legalized junkie, getting it on script...

I want to heal recover change my world.

Free my soul from the pain.

Do Doctors only work on logic?

Today's staffs apart from two are the worst mental health staff I have ever witnessed in my whole life, not that I have much experience being a newly qualified nutter. Hospitals are for the injured.

Mental hospitals are for the emotional injured, people with heavy shit on them, that is a burden on ones soul, people deal with the emotional pain differently, some take drugs, some get prescribed drugs, some block it out, some can level it out, some of us learn to face our fears, some battle it out but that is only my opinion with me now being a mental health patient.

The women in my dorm are really board today, our only break from the modality of the day is the cattle run for our cigarette break to get some fresh air. The rest of the time we are cooped up like battery chickens. All the women today have been extremely agitated whilst the staff argue between them who will take us for our cigarette break.

This is not good. I plonk myself down next to the security door, I am not moving till we get to go and get some air.

I tell the snotty little one. 'we are not in prison we have not committed a crime we are by law entitled to receive fresh air it is our basic human right'.

This is good for my mind, my body and my soul to breath in the clean fresh air. Plus I want a cigarette.

I get told we should be thankful we get taken out when they are short staffed.

Should we really be that thankful?

The nurse then barks at the woman who dared to speak, that we are lucky we even get to smoke.

I secretly hopes she trips in her stiletto shoes when she goes out this weekend; Woman are drugged up with nothing to do all day. More fresh air in these places and maybe some light exercise wouldn't go a miss. If patients want to. I'm told there is art therapy, I will go to that.

I don't feel like I will recover in this place.

Have I got mental problems?

Witchcraft - Prayers - Sixth-sense - Psychosis.

I will have by the time I am released. I need some sleep! Escaped woman has slashed her arms to bits today after a staff nurse gave her a razor, do these people not communicate to each other over patients? She had managed to get hold of alcohol and went on a bender the woman will have a big come down lasting more than a day or two especially with her being on other medication, she should not have been allowed the use of a razor until the blues pass. She had been left without bedding all day, so she is unable to rest, left to wonder around the ward in pain until the staff change over. When the staff changeover, the night shift immediately puts bedding on her bed for her, so she can rest.

Give me the squat back; I will never complain again I say to my guide.

Night 6

I've received permission today that I will be getting freedom for air and will be allowed off the hospital grounds for an hour each day.

I am going outside. I feel like a big girl now!

I have not the faintest idea where I will get to and still make it back in an hour, maybe I should leg it become a nutter on the run. We are miles from anywhere so without any cash on me, my plan for escaping gets squashed but I can get out of this ward and get some fresh air in my lungs.

Everything has been reasonably calm in here today, no self harming, no tears or violent outbreaks.

I have been told by a few patients that I am too calm.

To calm!

And that the staff will represent that to me being ill and keep me in here longer.

I don't care I shall now carry on in the state of calmness.

I ask myself should I create a fuss just to prove I am not mentally unwell, no way said the voice I am cured with being in a cell.

I have been in here six days. I have already read a few books it would be better if there was a garden. I want out now. I feel calm yet very tired, my brain is mentally fried, there is no negativity attached to me, so I feel a sense of peace.

The corridor night walker as I now call her is a ex prostitute, she walks up and down the corridor at night, medicated out of her mind. I've no idea what her story is, she is lost and she is stuck, trapped in her fears, too scared to face the suppressed memories, the suppressed emotions, still clinging to the piece of her soul that is carrying the burden, the weight of whatever she has suffered. she walks up and down the corridors in the trip of her past, looking for punters numbed in the darkness. Her head completely fucked! Her mind gone.

Night 7

I slept last night for nearly eight hours. Get a bit more sleep in and I might be able to blag the doctors to go let me go home.

I pray... get me out of here I've had enough.

With nothing to do and nowhere to go sleeping makes time less painful, each hour passes by slowly and with no privacy allowed during the day you start to get on each others nerves. The curtain around the bed must remain open.

Why am I not allowed to close my curtain and sleep I have been diagnosed with sleep deprivation and psychosis. I need to sleep, meditate and heal in private, why do I have to do everything out in full view. I am in hospital to recover, to heal, to be repaired?

Even with the curtain open I slept on/off for most of the day.

I feel free from pressure free of stress.

I feel like I will recover from this tiredness that has had me in its claws that dug in deep. I will shake off this cold. I feel free, my mind is clear free from death. Free from pain.

Night 8

I'm now getting of plenty of sleep… I wake up but I'm still worn out, absolutely knackered, still physically drained with no mental energy.

I look around and I see things as they are, it feels amazing, no ghost, no devil workers no soul suckers, evil spirits or underworld entities. I wonder where they have gone.

The fear has now vanished. There is a sense of peace surrounding me.

Can a person bounce back from months of hell and mental torture in seven days?

Did I keep my faith?

I feel liberated. Free your mind and the rest will follow. How very true.

Night 9

Cured I want out now!

I pray… I would like somewhere peaceful to help me heal so I can grow and flourish.

The younger girls who live here are finding different ways to entertain themselves, the doctors can section us so we are not allowed to leave but there is nothing for us to do.

Emotionally torn and nothing to do but to sink further in the dark getting sucked down back in the shit. Get used to the medication, then take more medication.

Why?

It did cross my mind to try and teach the women in my dorm some spiritual healing, or help them to start to meditate, a few simply breathing exercises to try and regain balance. I could set up a yoga class, if I knew all the positions. I thought this to myself but I do not intend on staying for much longer.

When you are sat on your backsides everyday you become even more energy less, so today each one is trying to outdo the other, acting foolish, being annoying, loud, they each try to shout louder, laugh louder, burp louder, fart louder, they try and sing the loudest to adverts on TV or who can scream the loudest at staff because they want more pain killers from the days previous when they all seemed to self harm.

I cannot stand the noise. months of living in silence has somehow affected my brain everything seems much louder. I have blinding headaches.

I repeat my prayer... get me out of here.

My blood test returned. No alcohol, no drugs - I feel like sticking my finger up at them. Have that!

I do believe the doctors are quite befuddled with my sudden spiritual recovery. I feel light headed!

I am going home tomorrow....hip hip hurray. I am getting out of this place.

Day 10

My Sectional detention has been reviewed; I am getting out of here.

I am diagnosed with acute and transient psychotic disorder and given a mental health care worker to help me at home.

I do a little dance and a song follows Oh you know it- I am getting out of here – I do believe they think I am mental but maybe I am.

I leave the hospital, I walk to my car that my sister had parked in the hospital car park and head back to the squat.

I do not believe it the twat has changed the locks.

For fuck sake.

Great, I can see my entire belongings in the squat through the letter box. I take the notice he has stuck to the door and I phone my aunt. I am now officially homeless. I do not care I am alive, I got no home, no business, but I am alive, I have life.

THE DOG THE CATS AND THE RADIO

I arrive at my aunts home, I have come out of hospital emotionally, mentally and physically drained, I have no energy, my life battery is flat. I am still getting a grasp of what happened.

'Was it real?' I ask my guide.

Did that just happen?

Ghosts are still around, I can feel the presence in the air, it feels calm, relaxed.

I keep getting eye blinding, sickening migraines, if I have to concentrate on anything that takes longer than thirty seconds. The pain pierces down the back of my head. I need peace and quiet I tell myself. My aunt's house is a busy lovely little place with people popping in and out during the day. My aunt happily bizzy bodying around after her cats and her dog. I usually love coming round here for my dinner, a natter and watching the telly with her.

But then it is not every day one gets sectioned then released from a mental institution now is it! The TV is so loud my head feel like I have just had a rocket lunched up my nose and it has exploded into my brain.

'Are you going deaf?' I ask my aunt

'No I am not, you cheeky bugger' my aunt laughs, everything seems so loud to me. Is it that my mind has popped, my brain has had such a traumatic time lately that I am super sensitive, I ask my guides 'or is it because I have just spent months living in silence and I need to adjust'?

The TV is on in the living room, the radio is on in the kitchen, I am unable to drive as that takes a lot more than the thirty seconds of concentration that I am capable of, so I go upstairs to the room my aunt has let me use until I am back on my feet again. I lie down.

I am grateful for a bed. My head feels heavy like it's been smashed in a motorbike accident and the paramedics cannot remove the helmet, I am supper sensitive to light, to noise, is this normal? I ask my guides. Will my mind recover?

This is not my aunt's fault, she did not change the locks on my squat but wants me, us to do the chores, come on jobs to be done she would sing, I just want to rest and recover not clean...

I still look like shit, I still feel like shit. It is really hard to explain to people what it is like when your head has just burst like a balloon, if I had broken my leg and people see it in plaster, they would know it was still on the mend, but I can hardly wrap a big bandage round my head now can I? One I would look like a complete twit and two people might want to put their signature on, like they do on a cast on your arm or leg causing me more pain and discomfort. So I help my aunt with the spring cleaning. I gut the bathroom, scrubbed the blinds from the kitchen and bedroom, scrub the kitchen window and the kitchen door, I move out the fridge and the tumble dryer and clean behind them.. I want to go back to hospital I say to my guides.

I'm only here to recover not stay permanently. I started to wish I would have stayed in hospital. Cos if the ghosts didn't kill me these migraines will.

I didn't need to ask my guides for assistance this time as one Friday night my aunt, who is a none believer of the spirit realm, went to see a medium with a friend, maybe she was trying to understand. My aunts son, her youngest child had died only seven months before. My aunt is grieving badly for her child. I had started taking to the dead, seeing the dead. People I once knew. Or maybe she also wanted to understand if I was in fact mentally insane or that I could be telling some truth.

The ghosts were back. The vision reappeared. The demons had returned.

The voice screamed loudly in my head.

GET YOUR STUFF AND GET OUT OF that FUCKING HOUSE...IF YOU DONT GET OUT I WILL COME DOWN THERE AND TAKE YOU... what??

YOU LAZY LITTLE BITCH YOU HAVE NOT DONE THE BATHROOM FLOOR...

What?

Who said that? Fear swept all over me...

I have spent the past few months ill, living in dog shit alley, I have just been discharged from hospital, I was supposed to be in recovery.

What was happening? I can hear voices again and the animals are getting jittery, freaked out by my presence. Can they sense something? Faces are starting to reappear. I panic and go back into fear. I am talking to the voices again.

I am freaking my elderly aunt out…

They say people like me are mad, seeing spirits and ghosts that are not real… but different cultures/religion since the beginning of time have also seen/spoke/ heard spirits from the other dimension. Native Indians call on their spirit guides for help and understanding-

Are they all mad?! Am I mad?

People go to mediums to communicate with loved ones who have now passed away and gone to the other side, is it the case that people only believe spirits are real when it suits them? I spend my day in meditation, I practice Tia Chi, I eat I read, I try to sleep, I have to leave.

I pick up my bag and I leave.

I go…

SOFA SURFING

Freshly freaked out and worn out. I just needed somewhere to crash out to chill. Friends offered me a place to crash, the ones I had left. Not many had a spare room even the ones that did wanted cash. but my friends offered me their sofa. This was to be when realized that I felt alone.

I travelled around for a few nights getting my head down wherever. I just wondered around going from place to place in a daze. Still totally freaked out over the experience I had recently encountered. Wondering around thinking where is it I go from here. Has my train stopped? Is this the final destination? I need some clothes and I need my passport voice said. I was not quite sure why or where I would be going.

What was my grand plan to be? I definitely needed some clothes; I was still wearing the big old tracksuit bottoms of controllers, tucked into my ugg boots, I make an mental note to make an appointment to see a solicitor and hopefully, I would be able to retrieve my belonging from dog shit alley. I have just my clothes what I was sectioned in, some pajamas, some toiletries and my bag.

I really did need some clothes.

I tried to think positive. I kept my faith; I still had cash left in the bank but no identification, no business and no address, I was now a mental patient, a freak of society, in scruffy far to big pants - she had everything once was the whispers that followed me around like a dark shadow you cannot shift. Voices in my head. Up and down on the roller coaster of life!

One morning cheesed off already with sofa surfing I get up get dressed and headed into town. Sod this I thought, I need a retreat a place by myself, somewhere quite. I went to the council and declared myself homeless to the homeless prevention team.

'Nothing we can do' the receptionist man said. 'But my landlord has changed the locks; I have got nowhere to live. He has locked me out and he still has all my belongings, my clothes, my furniture, everything, my ID. I've been in hospital, my landlord was supposed to bring the place to a certain acceptable standard not leave me homeless' I chipped at him.

The man looked at me with pity, poor woman look at the state of her was the look he had written all over his face, 'wait there' he ordered and departed quickly through the double doors into the back office. Not that I was going anywhere I had nowhere to go. I felt like chucking the towel in. Game over, self doubt set and match! The reception man then reappeared, with a slip of paper. 'I have arranged an appointment for you to be interviewed with a housing enforcement officer, Try your best to turn up on time' he said nodding his head at me, making sure I understood. Was he trying to telepathically let me know how important this interview was to be I wondered?

You see I am a mental patient so people talk to me differently, they look at me like I am stupid... a not right! They speak to me in a tone like I might also be deaf, possible dumb wondering to themselves has she taken this in or should I explain it to her again. I smiled and thanked him with a puzzled look on my face.

'It is against the law to change the locks, we call it an illegal eviction' the man told me with a smile.

Well I say an illegal eviction. Wondering what that would mean to a solicitor.

Sofa surfing is no fun, you feel in the way, your invading someone elses space. You have dumped yourself and the bag you carry round with you into somebody elses home, somebody elses peace. You become the mantel fixture in their quite time.

I travelled round for a few nights and then went to stay with two other friends in their tiny house with its lovely back garden. They both worked long hours so I had the house to myself most of the time. I was able to sit around and read during the day. I would help out with their washing, make the dinner for their return from work. I was cooking for myself anyway, It was ace to have a oven again.

These two people I will be grateful to forever, they refused to take any money from me, I was a no one, I was ID less. They made me feel welcome, we laughed, we hung out but I wanted a bedroom of my own, somewhere

where I could shut myself away from the world and heal my broken damaged wings. I had invaded their space for long enough.

Not having a bed of your own or your own little retreat, strips you of independence, I was now entirely dependent on other people compassion, thoughtfulness from others in itself can be very draining. You don't want to take up there precious space, the little space they have. So you shape yourself to live your life the way that the sofa owner lives their life. You get up when they get up, go to bed when they go to bed, but you are totally grateful that they have taken you in. The little injured bird with the broken wings that you have become...

No strength to fly off and nowhere to land even if you did have enough strength. I was emotional and mentally wiped out by this point.

You wanted change my guides would say. Yes I do know that, Thank you, I would reply.

I chatted to my guides and kept my faith that things would be OK, something would turn up. 'Go back to your aunts' voice had suggested.

'No I cannot go back; I don't want to stay there. It is not fair on her or me. I cannot expect her to live in silence or for her to turn the radio down, or tell her to stop singing because the fuse in my head popped. I want, no I need a little room of my own somewhere' I said to my guides. 'Somewhere I can relax, somewhere I can heal, somewhere by the sea that is what I need right now and I don't think my aunt really understand that I am freshly discharged ghost fearing nut case who now has a mental health team working with me.

I then got up and set off again to go into town, to see the homeless prevention team at the council and again declared myself homeless. They asked me questions on where I had been staying. The housing officer then called my aunt to check that I had been thrown out of her home.

The lady came back 'I have spoken to your aunt and according to her she would never see you on the streets, you have got a bed you're not homeless, sorry we cannot help' the housing officer then sent me away.

I spent more weeks sofa surfing at my sisters house. I went to see my aunt and explained that the council will not help me if they think I have got a bed at her house and explained why at the moment I cannot live there. I pleaded. Please tell the homeless team that you have thrown me out.

I went back to the council again and this time my aunt verified that I was no longer welcome at her house.

This phone call went down like a spit fighter plane crashing to the ground with my aunt, she was not happy that I decided not to stay with her and even more miffed off that other people were to think that she had chucked me out.

Living street life is no fun. I hoped and prayed that my train would stop before carrying on down and pulling in at that station. I prayed come on do me a favour, I want to come up now. I want to be somewhere peaceful and quite, out of the way have the summer off. Please find me somewhere that I could handle, somewhere that I can relax, after this head popper I have just had. Show me kindness... I deserve the summer off.

I attended the appointment with the housing enforcement officer at Blackrod council and gave her all the evidence I had, with regards to dog shit alley. Thinking that when I did my before and after recordings of the squat, I had no idea is going to be used in evidence. I showed the text messages that had been sent to me from Harry and my home video recording of Harry, him being totally unaware of my secret recordings like other people before that I had recorded, when the situation called for. She helped me arrange a solicitor to try and get access to the property to get back my belongings.

I used to see the street people, the tramps, and the homeless and was maybe was a bit snotty towards them. No one wants to stand next to them in the shop queue or sit next to them on a bench because they smell, they stink!

Do not give them any money I would think as they will only spend it on alcohol or drugs, they will not buy food...

Oh how naive I was to think this way, but that was me then and this is me now, virtually only inches away from joining the tramps, if it wasn't for my sister I would be joining them permanently in their world. Here was my new life, hanging out with the people that smelt. I was here, sat outside with no home, no bed not even a sofa. I can understand why these people drink alcohol and take drugs.

I would also need something, anything, so I could to try and get my head down. I thought gosh I would possibly try anything. Whatever I could get my hands on just to knock myself out, make myself unconscious. How can a person sleep night after night out here? In the cold, there is not a chance you can. It is impossible to get sleep, vulnerable and out in the open. When your lying out there, outside, freezing cold. Feeling the wind go straight through you, no bed for you tonight sweet cheeks, and get used to not having a pillow.

I had met a group of people one night whilst I went to sit and look at the sunset setting. To clear my head and gather my thoughts. An older man Roy came and sat next to me. Roy was a tramp. At first I was a bit freaked out, but we ended up chatting 'How did you end up living rough' I asked him, we chatted for a bit longer, we also both just sat in silence and watched the sunset over the horizon. Roy had lost everything when his wife died of a heart attack the day before their thirtieth wedding anniversary. One day he is high on life, within twelve months he had lost his job, lost his home and was now one of the stinky people I used to not want to stand next to in a shop queue.

Here we were now two of a kind. Homeless, me being even more grateful that I had my sisters sofa. Roy had a sad soul he told me the basics for surviving rough, If I ever slipped further down. I met Roy a few time during my visits to watch the sunset. We chatted and laughed, talking to a man with experience of how tragic life can become when you are trapped in the darkness. I also met a man and his wife one evening when I was watching the sun setting. The couple would come down to the sea front to also see the sunset and they would bring sandwiches and beer and hand them to the homeless that was sat around. My faith in people was being restored.

I didn't want to live life as a tramp but to be back in my posh apartment.

In my apartment I was screaming to anyone in a hundred mile radius that I wanted change but this change was not what I was expecting. This change was to change my life.

Wandering the streets finding somewhere dry to get your head down, Is shit. Now this is really really shit. I say to my guide.

Freezing down to the bones, lucky if you sleep with one eye open, I would be too scared to go into a real deep sleep. Bring back the squat!

I pray to my guides… I want to come up; I have gone down far enough. I would be taking drugs, I would need them, I would have to steal for them, I would have to sell my body to buy them and I don't want to do that. I want love and a house, a house full of love. I get the message of what you have been trying to tell me. I am sorry for being such an ungrateful bitch moaning about my apartment. I will never moan again if you bring me up. Please I would not survive out here without drugs. I the new street tramp the new homeless. Who am I to judge them or blame them, these are people living in freezing cold conditions, each with their own story, whilst we are tucked up on a cold winters night, their outside freezing to death.

Just please do not let me join them. I begged everyone. God, the source, My Guides, the Sun, the Moon, everyone even the pebbles on the beach I could not possibly take anything to chance. At least I still had my car and cash in my bank account.

Nobody ever wakes up, one random morning and thinks, right today is the day... yes... I can feel it. I have got that vibe going on. It will be today, yes definitely today. I have decided, I am going to have a god makeover, on this my life and go psychotic. One does not just turn around and say to their loved ones, Dear I have been thinking shit through and I would love to end up as a mental patient and lose everything!

I am going to face my fears have a little recuperation, revitalization and then I shall get some spiritual healing.

I spiritually cleansed in front of the patients and the staff. They all thought I was nuts. I think that I was a breath of fresh air, I didn't believe for one minute I was mad. I thought it was real.

Am I mad?

Sixth-Sense...That was only my diagnosis, although the doctor who sectioned me had a different view on the situation. Each patient thought I was madder than them, 'she is really chilled out, she must be off her rocker' and these rumors that was not really rumors, which to me was very refreshing, as they just told you what they thought straight to your face, no back stabbing in hospital with words.

I would council people on my bed, chat with the cleaners. I felt empathy.

Did I make myself homeless? Did I realize the magic in the power of thought when I dropped to my knees and demanded changed and I wanted fast changed.... All aboard... Choo choo!

So again I headed off to declare myself homeless. I was at the housing department quite early and I waited around for the doors to open at nine am. I was stood with my back leaning on the entrance door. This was a good move I told my guide. By the time nine am came and the doors were about to be open, at least a dozen or more people like me were wanting help to find somewhere safe to sleep. One young woman had a child in a pram with her, surly they haven't slept on the street? I prayed that if they did at least tonight they would hopefully be safe.

I walked over first in the queue 'I really cannot take the street life', I said to the receptionist 'I will end up being admitted back to hospital' I rather sternly told her 'now you wouldn't want that, would you?'

She told me to sit in the reception area and wait and she would try and get me a bed for tonight. I sat down and wondered where I was to be going next. The receptionist called me over, she had managed to get me a bed in one of the hostels. I would have to go there this afternoon for an interview and hopefully if everything is OK I should have my own bed. I thanked the receptionist for helping me and I thanked my guides for getting me a bed.

My interview was not the same as a job interview. I was questioned on why I had become homeless. I was tired and felt shit. I was asked more questions and was told the rules of the house. No alcohol and no drugs allowed in the rooms, there would be random room checks and a daily bin change.

I passed my interview and was offered a room. Pete the hostel manager showed me to my room, he unlocked the door of room nine. I was overwhelmed with gratitude. I looked at the single bed and wanted to chuck myself in it right there and then. Placed upon the bed was a towel, shampoo, body wash and a toothbrush, yet no toothpaste and a strange container for putting in used needles. I also now had a wardrobe and a sink and that was it. I was buzzing.

I really did appreciate my little room, in this dump of a place. It was like a haven. This was to be, for now, my new home. I will stay until I am ready to start again, have a fresh start, a brand new life I told myself. Whatever my new life is to be.

I had no idea as yet, I had not quite decided or made my mind up on where my life was going. All I knew that right now at this moment in time is that I wanted a summer off. A whole summer with no responsibility, no rent, no bills, no supermarket shopping, to be able to come and go as I pleased. I felt like a teenager again, who had moved back in to the parental family home..

Now where do I go from here?

For the first time in many years I felt free. Free to do whatever I liked, whatever I wanted. I could go anywhere, do anything but first thing first I told myself I would recover and chill. I felt safe in the security that everything I needed had been provided.

As I put my bag on the bed. I looked around the small nine ft by seven ft room with its woodchip wall covering, that must have been painted and re painted over fifty times since it was original hung many years before. My room, with a single bed, a single wardrobe and a sink, oh how I felt so incredibly grateful.

This was my room. The bed had a plain bright blue duvet cover. I was given a list of instruction explaining the procedures of the house. A great big, old hotel facing the sea, that must have been something special back in its glory days, was now a rundown hostel for us down and outs to get our heads down in comfort and safety each and every night. Every person had the same blue quilt cover and crisp white sheets. I locked my door, closed the blinds on the tiny window that over looked a main road, with the view of the moon and I prayed.

"Dear God, the source the main man, please surround me with a sphere of powerful, brilliant white light. Send the angels to protect me from all harm, and please send my Spirit Guides to guide me, guard me and keep away all negative influences thank you for bringing me to a safe place to stay, I am eternally grateful. With love Amen x"

I by now had also started blowing my God a kiss after my prayer x

As I lay on the bed with the peace that surrounded me, I would just chill out for hours and hours. I am here! This is real!

Life in the hostel had set times, breakfast is eight thirty am, Lunch is twelve thirty pm, Dinner four thirty pm, and supper nine pm. My sleeping pattern is shocking and if i miss any of the set times I am stuffed and have to wait for the next meal time to arrive before I can eat. Bedding to be changed every Monday morning, when fresh laundry from the week before arrives back. Again if one misses the change over you are stuffed and had to make do with the sheet you already had until the following week. The fire alarm drill would be every Wednesday morning at ten am. Now that was horrendous to be woken up to. On my first week nobody had mentioned anything about a drill. Tucked up in my bed and fast asleep, I was woken to a screeching noise. What the fuck is that... a second to register the noise to my brain... Fire alarm! I bolted out my bed, legged it down the stairs carrying what little possessions I had. To be informed that this was the weekly drill. My heart was pounding my ears ringing, I felt a proper idiot. With my room came the responsibility of cleaning our landings bathroom. Each room came with a job that had to be done every morning, this wasn't set in stone as long as it was kept clean so I cleaned the bathroom when I got up. I did not mind this job as I would have cleaned it before I used it anyway and at night when I was cosy, if I needed to urinate I just hopped on the sink and peed in it, hoping that it wouldn't fall off the wall. Each house mate also had to help wash the pots twice a month, easy living. The staff at the hostel was the best people in the world, they were kind, caring, compassionate, including the cook Lottie, she was the world's worst cook, everything was very bland or very greasy but she made the effort to cook it, I was grateful for food so I ate it. These are the people who would help me heal, recover, tell me this life is not forever it is just for now. Like this is forever? No. Don't destroy my summer by saying things like that' I would laugh.

I thanked God hourly for providing me some where safe. I am constantly happy. I would do a little thank you dance to show my appreciation. I am still going through the ball ache of the legal procedure to getting my stuff back so here I am in my new life, living out of a ruck sack in a hostel. And still I felt blessed.

I chatted with my guides full of hope and wonder, excited for what my new life would be. I started to think about all the other little coincidences that I had after a dream or vision or the feelings I get when my in built bullshit detector is bleeping 'WARNING!!'

When did I get everything so confused so fucked up, why did I care?

My old life - I started a new job in a new salon and mud travels, other new employee got the needle with me, just instance dislike after more shit has been thrown and I'm labeled a thief. I thought great here we go again. My boss asked me why I thought one of the other stylist had it in for me 'she has got marriage problems' I told my boss. turns out this was the very true. How did I know?

Holidaying years ago, I had a dream a vivid vision about cats, lots of cats different colors, different sizes just running away. As my friend and I was strolling down to the beach I told my friend about my dream, 'cats, not good' she said shaking her head 'not good'

'I'm gonna get robbed' I said out loud

'Not much you can do, were three thousand miles away'

And the conversation was closed
Robbed of what though I thought to myself.

Before I went on holiday I believe I had seen a ghost. Now I am having mad visions and seeing ghosts all the time, logically this is not real, because my mum said so after I told her that I saw a ghost when I was a kid. Not real! So one night after a hard days work I get in bed and just as soon as I lie down, placing my head on the pillow, I see my bedroom door slowly open. What the fuck!

A man walks in, I freeze in total fear, my whole body paralyzed, I cannot shout I can't scream, frozen solid with fear. He walks towards me, my head feel like it's pushing towards my headboard, casually he strolls next to my bed, stands next to me bends down to his knees and poof he is gone. But there were no puff of smoke.

Well I truly shit myself. It was one of the most frightening experience of my life! I couldn't fight - I couldn't try and run - I thought he was human. I was Frozen.

I jumped out of bed freaking out...what the fuck?

I was severely shaking. I was almost body popping into my dressing gown and as quick as lighting I got myself out that room. Woe...Did that just happen?

I then went on holiday. I had Weird dreams on holiday and what with seeing a ghost. I think I might be slightly mad. I return home a week later,after my holiday at early morning dawn, I throw my case down, looked around and felt extremely grateful that I had not been robbed. I Google dreams on cats.

Every religion has its own dream interpretation I had no idea what this meant.

Are ghost real?

Some say yes, some say not.

Confused, I was asking the universe what religion I belonged to as then I wouldn't be confused, back in the days when I was still finding my path.

I drift off to sleep. Suddenly I wake up, wide awake and alert. I lay there with my eyes wide open thinking; I feel a bit peckish, I think I will put a pizza in the oven. I get up, walk into the kitchen, my flat is in darkness and just as I am about to flick the switch to put the light on I hear a roar of smashing glass, followed by a big thud, eerily the kitchen light then comes on, I run to the bedroom, I can hear people running away and there is a rock, a big fuck off bolder on the floor, window glass all smashed to pieces. I call the police. Fuck this I am moving out. What were the cats about?

Before the court case I had a vision of three dogs jumping up at me, I had tried to run away but they followed me but no matter how much they barked they never bit me. When the mud started to get thrown, three nasty bitches set me up in my place of work, secret veil at work but I knew it was coming, I was in the salon of lethal substance, I felt the vibes it was in the air. I knew after I had gone back in the salon after they had at suspended me, then at first they tried to bribe me, pay me to leave, that it wouldn't be the end. But clever me, I had recorded our meetings, on my mobile phone. I went back to work, after fighting against the three dogs of my dreams. I walked back in to the salon thinking fuck you, but why did I do that? I had already secured another job? Because I knew I was in the right.

What a pair of tossers they were making me sit upstairs in the staff room. I can laugh to myself now; they did this so my clients would think I was still off work. Suspended for gross misconduct. My first day back in the salon the bosses confiscating my phone because they know I love to record, so when the two lovers had checked my bag on the morning of my return to work, I had already set a code on my mobile phone and had taken in a dictator phone. I prayed my dictator phone wouldn't drop out of my pocket. I was slightly Paranoid every time I turned it on. I was continually going to the loo, one to make sure my clients saw me on the property and two to check my tape, the little mini tape recorder, I had shoved in my pocket was doing its job. I am mad!

One of the junior walked into the staff room and looked at me like I was shit, removed her mobile phone from her bag, then spent ages on it chatting to her boyfriend, her being the elegant beautiful swan that she was, she who was allowed her phone, me being shit was not allowed to use my phone at work anymore. I had recorded it all. Am I mad? I laugh to this day now that I had a dictator phone in my pocket; I was taking nothing to chance and as always, like other little things that come my way someone had just given it to me days before I was due to go back to work. Suspension over ruled!

I thought about all the strangeness, the things that had been weird that went on around that time in my life time and think how much mud does stick.

Nothing made sense when things happened and nothing makes any sense now... sense... should it make sense? I try to think of other dreams other things that have happened, other warnings, other signs. I tell myself I am mad!

I had told friends about my visions, my dreams, I would sit going through dream interpretation books and as soon as it was a decent hour to ring someone up, I was straight on the phone to a friend, I swear I have seen a ghost. Are ghost real?

Now here I am sitting in the hostel thinking what happened, my fear of ghosts, my fear of death, my fear of letting go. The guilt and shame I felt when I went sleepwalking, anything could of happened to my children.

Was this the start of the ghost train?

Was it real, I had told people, does that make it real?

Was this when logic joined the crew?

It is all just crazy talk.

Logic gets over ruled.

We all have our different problems in the hostel there are some good people, who are just down on their luck. Some are fresh from prison on conditions of bail, some are alcoholics, others crack heads or heroin addicts. Me I came from the mental hospital - the nut house! Different people thrown together to became a massive house share.

I now have an address so I can apply for employment support allowance, I being chuffed to bits with myself that I have always paid my national insurance contributions. I managed to get my belongings back and put everything in storage. And I mean everything, I take the carpets I paid for, the light fixtures and the blinds. I start house hunting and also put my name down for a house with Blackrod Council.

I either spend my days relaxing on the beach chilling in the summer sun or I spend time alone relaxing in my room. The staff turned a blind eye to me lighting candles, incense sticks or when I cleansed my room with sage. I managed to set the fire alarm off a couple of times whilst I was smudging. It really was like a teenager's bedroom. Apart from we are not allowed any posters on the walls and no visitors were allowed past the main reception.

There are no kettles or irons allowed in the hostel bed rooms. All facilities are provided for in a communal room, there are two massive adjoining rooms, one room has computers with internet access, a dart board. Everything is here to make drinks, tea, coffee, milk and juice; this is provided from seven am until twelve am. This is where on a wet raining day the house mates of the hostel would all hang out. The other room had a big TV in, with sofas and chairs and tables with lamps just like a living room you would have at home. Different people from different walks of life all sat comfy watching TV.

It is here in my hostel room I truly started believing in my Faith. But what Faith, I am not religious, I have never been christened, I do not believe in conventional religion but I do believe in God my God. I prayed, I meditated, I day dream my world.

I prayed to the Angle of Faith please help me keep my faith, just in case I have a weak moment I am asking in advance. Thanks amen with love Maggie x

The sun is shining

The sea blue and green

Waves calmly making the way into the vastness

The sky in the distance, meets with the waves

This is the day, my soul shall be saved

The beauty, the wonder, the joy of it all

The excitement inside,

I've watched myself fall,

I pick up the pieces of what once was my life,

A brand new beginning a fresh new start,

The old and the new are now drifting apart.

Was my spirit guide communicating with me through words?

I sit down and I close my eyes, I breath in deep breaths that fill my stomach with air like the balloon that is slowly filling up. I have a conversation in my head. It is still my voice that asks the questions then my voice that answers them again. This is so confusing I grumble to my guide.

Days and weeks roll on, months go by people come and go from hostel life. Nothing stays the same with change.

I rent my own house. My new landlord is now Blackrod county council. It has everything I asked for in my spell. Well nearly everything, I cannot fit a dining table in the kitchen, but I have my own driveway. I strip the whole house of wallpaper, and paint each room. I have the carpets laid and the light fixtures hung. This is now my home for life if I choose it to be. Vision still appearing and I still have no idea what they mean but there are not scary anymore.

THE SHIFT

F ear of change.
I ask myself Am I mad? Questions and more questions. And one by one
the universe steps in –

?

I pray to the angle of faith –

I cannot put my finger on it I cannot see the truth.

What is it I feel – do I not belong to you?

The blonde little girl, bright green piercing eyes, burying the guilt I
have deep inside.

What are you saying?

I do want to know the truth.

The years that go by my love is for you.

I come across sayings, philosophies, articles, books, I believe these are
signs. These are the answer to my question. I have joined thousand of other
nutters who believe they have their very own God- Old religion, faith, my
pagan way, my God - Mother Nature, where I'm free to do what I want
whenever I like... love, peace and happiness... I shall toast to that! I am
surrounded by my highest spirit guides that help to keep me in a peaceful
calmful tranquility.

I look in the mirror I look completely knackered, drained, yet I am
glowing. My battery for life is plugged in and on charge. I just want to lie
down somewhere and not think, no noise, no distraction. Be in bliss.

My mind recalls a story, I cannot remember where from, but it came
into my head like a magazine, quick flash:

Native American story teller... The elders have sent me to tell you that
now is a rushing river and this will be experienced in many ways. There
are those who would hold on to the shore...there is no shore. The shore is

crumbling, push off into the middle of the river, keep your head above the water, look around to see who else is in the river with you and celebrate.

THOUGHTS – IDEAS – MANIFEST – DETACHMENT

Have I suffered death, this concept might seem scary... Letting go of what is known, for the unknown.

It's a bit like going on a roller coaster ride you know it's perfectly safe but at the same time anticipation – you spend hours queuing, patiently going uphill to the ride, taking a couple of steps at a time. Then everyone around stops, sits down and waits. To all get up again and plod slowly along. Waiting for their turn on the ride, this particular train ride.

When I put my mind back, to dog shit alley when Guru Meditation appeared on the screen of my laptop. A big dark figure stood in the corner of my room. Was it because I was facing my fears? Was it real is it just an illusion?

Can we each create our own existence, our own world?

Now I've been homeless and stripped of security, knowing how hard it can be to let go. Let go of fear, blame, guilt,

I accept it – I release it. Some things may not seem pleasant – I accept it – I release it. Some things you may not understand – do not analyze it, don't panic – I accept it – I release it. Do not try and replace things, just work on release. Every now and then a fear pops up. I accept it – I release it.

I ask myself over and over. What has just happen? What the fuck!

I begged and pleaded for change to every god, goddess, angle, guide and ancestor that I could. To the Sun, to the Moon, to Divine Nature. I have learnt to respect my god, my faith and with it, it has made me extremely grateful for the small things in life.

I pray to my angles, my God and my guides. Some random thoughts pop up in my mind, I don't like that thought – I accept it- I release it. I do not hold on to it, I am now free of shit.

Shit free is the way to be!

In true form of my body, my spirit and my mind - To be as one.

I ask my guide 'does my fear of death have something to do with what has happened in a past life?' Or the trauma of losing loved ones in this life, have I been storing up suppressed emotions? Did I experience death living with dead in dog shit alley?'

Who starts contacting the dead. I must be mad! Leave them in peace. My guide tells me. I try but them, the ghosts will not leave me alone.

Remove triggers of past behaviours that are no longer supporting your higher self your soul, as those triggers need to go, ask for help.

Was this my answer?

Your soul needs love and laughter and the light guiding you in the right way, feel the sun on your face, feel the pleasant feeling, feeling at one, knowing that however hard it seems to be, trust in your guides work with the angles.

PARANOIA DEATH

FEER

Relationships   Success   Failure

S eeing ghosts and hearing spirits terrorized me. I can laugh now but I was traumatized living in dog shit alley, opposite a funeral parlour with the lingering soul sucking vultures.

'Why?' My guide asks

'I felt uneasy, I didn't like it'

'You have been vibrating at a lower frequency' replies my guide. 'caught up in negative suppressed emotions, always fearing the worst, you have stored up far too many negative thoughts that have been pushed down into the cardboard box at the back of your mind, the box was full and was unable to store anymore' guide carries on 'The road to enlightenment can be tough'.

'So have I got mental issues?

'I don't know' guide laughs 'but if you're worried seek medical advice'.

Great I thought even my guides think I could be mad!

'Crazy things happen when I close my eyes'

'You are not grounded'

'I hate being grounded as a child it was punishment' I say

'You were also scared of the dark. You have to climb higher but you fear heights...Rebellious wilful... you must ground yourself. Each experience has been a lesson in learning, you wanted change and change is what you have got. We are here to help, to guide, not to force you, surround yourself in the love and protection, use this time to help yourself heal, helping you feel at peace. Work on your inner balance' he assures me. 'Learning to use the right side of your brain-instead of none'

Going through the shift, strange things are happening, I ask a question. I don't ask millions of questions I ask the same question a million times... Am I Mad?

'Be Careful, things will now be given to you Books, you must read. Numbers, take note. Music, listen. You will learn to tell the difference, this is learning just have fun, don't sweat, if you make a mistake just laugh, don't be so serious. We also like to tease you to see how you work things out' guide informs me 'whilst you are still learning, ask for help'

I say a prayer.

I cast a spell

Let my most loving and top ranking guides, the big man in the sky, the source, God and the Goddess, all the angles surround and protect me whilst I sleep amen x

Numbed by my heart pain overload, that was tearing away part of my soul. I salvaged some sense, I turned my thoughts clear. I was drawing in love that I didn't want here, making hurt their entire fault. I was carrying the hurt and the anger throughout the years, the resentment, distrust, tantrums and tears. I prayed one day that you would return, you would answer my questions the truth I would learn. Unlock me from the prison I have kept myself in. I couldn't go forward I couldn't go back. The memory of pain was like a viscous attack, it came like a sword slicing right through my heart. penetrating my stomach like we was never apart. So I have accepted and I have released all of my pain, without judgement or bitterness or placing the blame. Who knows what my life will now have in store, being released from the prison that was once before. To love again is all I ask, to be free from the shit is my ultimate task.

With love x

I have spent the past five days in my bedroom, only coming out to nip to the shop and eat.

I hear my Guides when they tell me to drink plenty of water to stop dehydration, eat plenty of fruit and vegetables, eat garlic it is god's natural anti biotic and keeps you grounded. Now is not the time to self doubt. I sneak out of the house late at night like a cat burglar on a secret mission. I go to the all night supermarket, I fill my trolley up with everything I need and head back home to my bedroom fully prepared for my time of incubation.

'Imagine a bear in hibernation, warm and cosy' voice teases.

I am now learning to accept it, to embrace it. I do a mirror check; I look tired, old, worn out, yet sleepy, dreamy, loved up.

Do not rely on someone else for you happiness and self worth, was the message that I was given.

I pray to angel Uriel for some Reiki healing and I lie on my bed. Feeling my body grounded like someone is stood on me pushing me further and further deep into the ground whilst at the same time feeling as if my body is floating. I check to see if my eyes are closed, yes my eyes are closed but I see the visions, the colors. I feel the deep sense of inner peace.

I listen to my inner voice that tells me I am now spiritually cleansed. Keep doing Tai Chi, work on your breathing. You need to recover, you was not eating, you was not sleeping, you was facing your fears. You have faced your fears. Now you are healing from those fears from which you have faced. Painful experiences take time to heal, allow for time, do not rush. Thoughts are slowly being removed.

I am working on balancing my chakras an ancient form of healing:

Seventh/ Crown: Located at the top of the head: Its function is understanding. Its inner state is: Bliss. Its colour is violet and its planet is Uranus. Its stone is amethyst. Its meditation is: I understand. Balancing this chakra is said to give vitality to the cerebrum and affects the development of psychic abilities. Energies: air, meditative, intuition, promotes thought.

Sixth/ Third Eye: Located in the centre of the forehead, above the eyebrows: Its function is seeing, intuiting. Its inner state is: I know. Its colour is indigo and its planet is Jupiter. Its stone is lolite. Its meditation is: I see. Balancing this chakra helps psychic perception and balances the pineal gland. Energies: air, meditative intuition.

Fifth/ Throat: Located in the throat: Its function is communication, creativity. Its inner state is: Synthesis of ideas into symbols. Its colour is bright blue. Its planets are mercury and Neptune. Its stones are sodalite, blue lace and agate. Meditation on: I speak. Balancing this chakra is important for the speech and communication areas of the brain. Energies: water, calming sooths relaxes.

Forth/ Heart: Located in the centre of the chest: Its function is Love. Its inner state is: compassion, love. Its colour is green. Its planet is venus. Its stones are: green/pink stones-peridot, rose quarts and malachite. Meditation on: I love. Balancing this chakra is important for the circulatory system, heart and thymus. It also affects spiritual love, compassion and universal oneness. Energies: water, calming sooths relaxes.

Third/ Solar Plexus: Located in the area above the navel: Its function is: Will, power. Its inner state is: Laughter, joy, anger. Its colour is yellow. Its planets are mars and the sun. Its stones are: Amber, topaz and citrine. Meditation on: I do. Balancing this chakra is associated with calming emotions and frustrations, easing tensions. Energies: Fire energizing, charging, lends energy.

Second/ Sacral: Located in the lower abdomen, genitals and womb. Its function is: Desire, sexuality, pleasure, procreation. Its inner state is: Tears. Its colour is orange and its celestial body is the moon. Its stones are: Coral and carnelian. Meditation on: I feel. Balancing this chakra is associated with sexual vitality, physical power and fertility. Energies: Fire, energizing, charging.

First/ Root: Located in the base of the spine. Its function is: survival and grounding. Its inner state is: Stillness and stability. Its colour is red. And its planets are earth and Saturn. Its stones are ruby, onyx, obsidian. Meditation on: I am. Balancing this chakra gives energy to the physical body, controls fear, increases overall health and helps in grounding. Energies: Earth, grounding, focusing, centering.

The symptoms I am experiencing at the moment are memory loss, fatigue, cramps, pins and needles in my legs, feet and my hands. My old way of thinking is starting to get erased and new healthy patterns are starting to slip in their place. I am surprising myself of some of the things I say. I am learning to laugh and smile again... I am being guided by the love. I've got no energy. I chill out on my bed and I drift off in to a complete state of oneness, the imagery drifting across my mind, sweeping in and out in the background the colour purple. I can see but still in stiletto forms as if there just strolling in and out, I check my eyes. They are closed.

Positive messages start to pop in my mind during meditation, who wrote the quotes originally I have no idea, I do not ask, I just listen to the advice that is being given.

Deal with thoughts as they arrive – do not dwell in the thought. Do not make the thought out to be bigger than its is. This is not a band-aid this is love healing.

I am still learning, so I take great comfort in knowing things are coming, my head feel like a electrical power station zapping energy into my mind... Come on lads time to get this ship running again, is what the captain in my mind encourages his crew. You cannot build a new ship from old wood, remove the dead wood, we are building a new ship.

SWING

Death and Rebirth ... 'out with the old' the captain carries out his commands.

I have, as I believe we all do have a spirit guide....Do we all have a spirit guide? Do you have a spirit guide? My spirit guide looks like a cross between a caveman and a gorilla but he appears a lot shorter and he has a bushy and quite a long tail that stands erect. I call him by the name of Safehouse. I also have my ego - stubborn little bugger I call her mountain goat. I have my logic- good old sense. Then me, my highest self – my truest form My soul.

My main man, my most loving, protective and supportive spirit guide who is always with me and is a far as I believe, always has been around. I just needed to ask for help. I am privileged I have been able to interpret. And as I see through my eyes, that this is what he looks like. I am saying Safehouse is a he; he could be a she or a mixture of both male and female form.

I imagine this is a scene going on with the captain in my mind, as I cannot hear him; Mountain goat, logic, Safehouse and me is enough of a community in my head, this can be proper confusing but I am learning to live with my guides and the separate voices. But I could possibly be just mad.

A psychiatric patient or sixth sense.

Understanding being creative, realizing, accepting - moving forward be confident enjoy - shifting, create your world.

I ground myself every morning. I think of happy times the lovely memories, I burst out in little songs and I dance. I love sitting by the sea.

DELIGHT – TEMPERANCE – INSPIRED –REST

I ground. I pray.

Let peace be with you and me

I love and forgive myself

I love and forgive others...

With love, amen, lots of love and kisses x

I never really know how to end my prayer, I say to my guide.

'Whatever feels the most natural go with the flow of how you feel if it feels good it's all good'.

AM I MAD?

Even though no sane person would be willing to put themselves in such a position, healing often occurs in places of ambiguity conflict, this is a true contradiction to what is life. Those who lose win, those who come last are first those who give receive; those who brave the dark became lighter. Note from safe house

Am I coming out in the sun?

'Like a sunflower baby' says mountain goat.

I will love and forgive others I will love and forgive myself… my little morning mantra. Forgive others - can I really forgive?

I can see why people would think I am mad, mental … stay away from her, she is mad… Maybe I am mad, but if been mad means I am extraordinarily happy. I will stick with staying mad as life before was shit now it is not.

Now back to your lesson, your mission is accomplished your fear of darkness has been erased, you now have love peace tranquility.

Each and every year you will feel brighter with health, glowing my dear, let the light that surrounds you be your energy flow, you've come so far you're just too stupid to know.

My higher self is now setting standard!

I need to be at one but I also need to be able to switch off for privacy.

Being in love with yourself, is not big headed, being confident is not being cocky, be independent, be successful, be smart, dress smart, look smart. Feel smart! Where did that beautiful child go!? – Instant connection – smile.

I am still taking baby steps at the moment, I have decided to not make any decisions. I am going to see what comes my way and check how things pan out; Creating the life I want to live in as it is not yet created.

My world is becoming clearer a lot calmer; I am finding things I love!

Me: I love being outdoors… I danced on the sea wall on a cold windy afternoon in December, feeling the mist of the sea on my face the wind running through my hair letting my spirit roam free.

'I do like to be beside the seaside, we must visit as many beaches around the world as possible' chats mountain goat.

I will agree to that!

So we have got mountain goat, my higher self, my guides – always my most loving highest guide, just to be on the safe side and then my logic.

THIS IS NOT REAL

WARNING!!!

Not Real

'So why does it make so much sense then?' I question my logic.

'It is just a illusion'

'So if life is an illusion and this is my life does that not make it real?'

Make it real, make it happen, create your day, feel happy in the know.

Moving forward into the silence, moving into peace, off to meet my higher self, which is where I am going. I can hear her talk, I am her My Soul, I am she and she is me, and together we are one.

I have also started to rationalize. I have now surrendered all control to my higher self, all control meaning I do what she says. Mountain goat is now the second voice. I close my eyes and I am starting to see and when my eyes are open I am alert to my surroundings.

Thoughts arise then sayings pop up, usually the saying comes as my answers.

Sometimes good things fall apart so better things call fall together and how true. I was not complete in my old life. I wanted something to change but I wanted radical change, being in a mental hospital I think was only to confirm what I already am.

I am now officially a mental patient to some I am a nut job, the crazy lady who sees things that are not there..

Being homeless, a real life down and out, I have been to the bottom of society lived it breathed it, I have become humble. I have met some good people and moved away from the fakes. Some once had a dig at me about Karma; you get what you give.

Wait till it is your time to hit the shit baby, you best get praying!

My life is good in the hood.

What I have experienced because it was real to me has helped me to have more understanding more compassion towards myself., towards others.

No one can truly understands or really know what it feels like to be down there, living with the dead and the human vampires that suck on your soul. Leaving you with no energy. How can anybody truly understand or even bother to try. Who really cares?

What a god dam crazy year it has been. I knew what was happening. You just know when you know!

I was on the wrong path of life? Did I go to dog shit alley to experience death? I ask my guides,

I always use the right names of course, my most loving and highest guides.

I wanted to change my path. I wanted to get off the shitty dirt road that life once was, and you cannot reach second base with your foot on first, so something needed to go.

For leafs to reach heaven, roots first must touch hell…is this true?

In this life you've got to go for it and aim for the moon because if you fail you will land between the stars. Create a life, a happy life, one that when you wake up in the morning you shout out GOOD MORNING UNIVEARSE with a great big cheesy grin on your face, smile be happy for the simple privilege of being alive, I am alive and life is good. Yes it is all good in the hood, being safe and warm, clothed and fed.

That once upon a time I was little miss sensible.

Prim and proper in my youth.

Sensible in my Twenties

Hardworking in my Thirties

Psychotic in my forties

Does life really begin at forty?

Or fifty or sixty or whenever you want it to begin.

COMMUNICATING WITH MY GUIDES

After months of thinking I could be or at the very least thinking there is a slight possibility that I am mad. Psychotic. I tried alternate therapies, I had reiki healing and reflexology. I paid for this privately.

What was I thinking moving in to the squat?! renting a bed in the nut house, being homeless stripped of everything, yet throughout my whole experience I have been surprised at people's different reactions.

Get back to nursery and learn how to spell one shit slinger had said to me not long after my release from hospital. My brain was still trying to recover from the trauma it has just been through. In response to that mountain goat wanted to bite back- get to the dentist your teeth look like they belong in the mouth of a horse but I kept my mouth shut.

I have finally sussed it; well let's say I think I've sussed it, somewhere in my tiny mixed up brain, something might of possibly finally clicked. When I attended the spiritual church and Bob mentioned the different sensations you get, the feeling you get, the feeling you just know. When I hear the voices; that all have the same voice as me in my head this can be proper confusing, who is saying what. I am not so switched on, I can get mixed up but when I am switched on I can always tell who's who in the community in my head!

Do we all have a fear of change? Do we fear death? I ask question after question and still more questions.

And one by one the universe steps in —It takes effort and practice to connect with your higher self and your spirit guides, meditation brings wisdom, lack of meditation brings ignorance Safehouse tells me. You're surrounded by your highest spirit guides that keep you in a peaceful, calmful tranquility.

Really you are joking me, did I just hear that?

I look in the mirror I look ill. Why do I still look like shit? I ask
THOUGHTS – IDEAS – MANIFEST – DETACHMENT
Death and Rebirth this concept might seem scary...
'Oh I am scared alright' I reply.
Letting go of the known for the unknown.

You have spent your time queuing for this next roller coaster ride, you
have been down to the bottom, now its time for you to go up to the top, keep
your faith and know it's perfectly safe but at the same time your anxious –
you spent hours queuing, years even for this particular ride, you are just
about to sit in the seat- Fear sets in.

'Get on the seat' my guides reassure me
'feel safe in the knowledge you are completely safe'.

You don't know what to expect but you know that once you get on the
seat your ride will be thoroughly enjoyable and pleasant

Get on that seat!

I've been fighting demons, In battle to save my soul. I have been to hell
and back and I tried to go to church, for you to tell me now after all this it
now game over, time is up?

TICK TOCK

Final countdown!

I am grounding myself much deeper, a deeper connection is happening
in my bedroom, my very own bedroom in my new house. With my garden
receiving the sun from dusk till dawn and a five minute walk to the shop,
it is perfect. Everything I need to create a relaxing atmosphere has been
provided, crystals and stones keep coming my way. It seem like I have been
collecting things ready for my next phase.

Being homeless and stripped of security has made me extremely grateful
for the small things in life. I pray to my angles and my guides. I am learning
to face my fears –Some random thought pops up in my mind, I don't like
that thought – I accept it, I release it.

'Essentially know we are here' safehouse soothes me 'we will not
rush you'.

'You will not rush me, you have dragged me here kicking and screaming!
I reply.

Spiritual teaching is a better way of life.

I have painted my bedroom wall red for grounding my root chakra, I had no intentions of painting one wall red but as I went to buy paint my inner voice was shouting out go for red'.

Just as I need things, things arrive for me to complete my spiritual cleansing process. This has been going on way before dog shit alley. I wanted change. All I know it was I threw myself on the floor and I prayed, I prayed for change, I wanted help with change, I demanded change, I commanded change. I wanted to be able to live through my highest self. to free myself from the shit and remove the mud. Not to be holier than thou but in true form of my body my spirit and my mind. To be as one

Visions sweep in and out of my mind. I feel the deep sense of inner peace total happiness.

I have changed to calmness over anxiety, gratefulness over always wanting more, and faith over fear. I listen to my inner voice. I am discovering that my life is what I want it to be. I laugh and smile... I am being guided by the love.

I have got no negative energy bringing me down as I have removed all the blockages and I am taking each step day by day. Who knows what my future will bring. I am no longer in a rush, what will be shall be. I am content with me at this moment in time. I potter around my home and my garden, I ground, I meditate then I chill out and accede to drift off in to a complete state of oneness,

The images drifting across my mind
Sweeping in and out the background,
Brilliantly bright so colourful.
I can see a great deal but nothing at all,
Still they stay in stiletto form
Strolling in and out
Wonderfully free
I am free from fear.... I am free from doubt
Free from anger, resentment and pain
My soul and I together again.
I've got nowhere to go and nothing to do but admire the visualization
I check my eyes. They are closed.
Simplicity - Radiant - Bewitching
Blow in the wind seeds of change, water watch grow and nurture with
love

I know who I am and make choices based on what I know to be right for me. I am supported in life through all my choices to do well and share the light of love. My body supporting me in living a creative and happy life. I am open to the spirit of life which carries me beyond my original limits to a higher more creative space. Each day I am thankful for all the opportunities for the growth and development that have come my way. I am grateful for the challenges that have taught me who I truly am.

I love life. I love me.

I have happy thoughts and daydreams. I have stripped away old emotions. old thought patterns.

I have kept my faith I have stayed true to myself.

The piece of my soul that split off taking all the past hurts that was to deep of a wound to deal with has now return.

Accepting those hurts and releasing

I ACCEPT…I REALESE

Get out be happy, create your world. I close my eyes visions appear but I have also learnt how to switch off. I do believe that I am learning how to swim. I delved deep into my soul to remove the shit, the mud and the dead wood. I have released the anger, the guilt, the resentment, the rejection and the fear on my search to find myself.

Right now I feel right and exact

We are as we are,

I am as I am.

Me my soul, together we shall celebrate

You shall never know how far you can fly unless you spread your wings!

I love you – who me?

Yes you

Separation not anymore

As when fear came calling love answered the door x

AM I MAD?

My life right now just does not seem real. I look back on the things I that I refuse to accept in a bid not to be controlled and to live my life as I choose to be -a free spirit.

When did marriage become a prison and man became the jailer?

I thank my god. I am not in a religion that I would be stoned to death right now for the many sins that I have committed. Why should I as a woman not have the same rights as a man? Why should I wait to get married before I make love or enjoy sex? Why did God give us the free gift such as the orgasm if we are not allowed to use it? I do not see the point. Its healthy, I as a woman have sexual desires that need fulfilling. No sex before marriage I really do not want that religion or should I say that religion did not want me in their church,. so I do not care what they say. Some people may choose to wait until they do get married that is their choice: Free will. For me I will live in the happiest state of sin that there can be. Only God can judge and my world is full of happiness and love so I do not think I am being criticized by God on a few meaningless sexual encounters.. If I am going to give up my single status and commit myself to loving one man that man better prove he is worth my love:

Sex is not love...

Lust is good fun...

Love is amazing.

I tried to go to go to many different churches, one church put the fear of the death chill throughout me and I was already in a serious fucked up head tripping mode.

The congregation left. The loving church click, they walked out! In the middle of my battle with the devil himself, living the trip. Freaking out in church, just as every normal sane person likes to do now and again. Not!

164

Did they not realize I was having a serious soul retrieval, a breakdown, a psychotic attack! and I was not just some chaotic totally demented ice queen of death. gate crashing their Sunday morning church service for fun and I hadn't just nipped in to ruin their morning.

I had to hit the breaks in the middle of my high speed train ride. I had to try and push the pause button momentarily trying to come back to reality. Because I was gobsmacked at the church goers actions... you call that living in love! I do not believe it is. Conform to the rules is all bullshit and bollocks. It is all about love.

Lifting my head up I start looking around and people are staring at me, yes I can understand that I had a bit of a mission going on, but they were all glaring at me with their eyes wide open like I was some kind of outcast, or wolf person, half woman half beast but predominately smellier and definitely on a bad hair day. The whole church became silent. It was spooky, I was spooked right out and in a daze with the hundred or more people that were staring at me. Then someone spoke 'Remove her' he shouted to the man of the church. I was gobsmacked each person after that man, the man that had spoken, started calling me for me to be removed.

Now I had been kicked out of a few places in my mission for change, usually it is when I am dealing with some kind of emotional shit get to drunk and get told to go home. I can handle that, but here I was getting kicked out of a church!

No way. that wasn't real! Yes that was real!

I mean it if they, the congregation felt uneasy with my presence you can imagine what extra state that put my already fucked up head in to.

They all just huffed and puffed and walked out. Now if that is not a head fuck, when your heads already fucked, what is? *Oh my god they think I am the devil!* 'I am not the devil' I started yelling at the people leaving. I did this in an attempt to try and sway the congregation to convince them to stay, that they did not need to abandon their morning service. I failed.

'I cannot remove this child she is a child of god' said the church man, himself not daring to approach me, his cross in hand as if I was about to grow fangs slither into a dark shadow and suck out his soul.

Silently they all stood up, each and every person keeping their eyes firmly on me, just in case I was the devil and I tried to make a move and grab on to their soul, they fucked off and left, just walked right out. These god fearing Christians who attend church every Sunday were more pissed off that I was having a serious soul retrieval session, mental breakdown a complete loss of reality going on. And they all walk out. Or better put they rushed out, I thought some might be in training for the Olympics.

I mean they could have offered help!

Instead they were pig ignorant, narrow minded and completely mortified that I had so rudely disrupted their Sunday morning service of hymens, praising the lord and having great plans on how they would save the world. Yet the whole congregation walks out. Do churches not usually try and drag you in?

But in fairness to the congregation I did arrive at church looking like I was a sister to the darkness of death, who was having a tantrum and refusing to return to my coffin, screaming from the top of my lungs at the floor. 'I am not going down there' whilst I was jumping up and down on the floor like an utter nutter in a desperate attempt to save my soul.

Different churches were all different, some showed a bit of loving and support; one man of god gave me a wooden cross he had blessed.

Bless him x

A churchman blessed my car and gave me a bible he had blessed.

Bless him x

I never got around to getting blessed myself for the reason I totally know the answer to. I sat in the sun, then chilled under the moon. I know my Pagan path is the one that suits me. Was I pushing and testing my belief system, did I have a belief system or was it an illusion?

Beep beep baby... an illusion!

I have faith. I would say I have experienced the ultimate trip ...the further you go down the higher you get to go up.

The life that was shit.

I wanted things to change and I must have meant at the time being heartbroken, losing someone your truly love is a devastating experience it a cycle you go into denial, then you grieve. you become angry, angry at the world, unable to cope with the emotional pain that is tearing at your soul. Deep you search for a solution sometime to fix it, something to temporarily stop the bleeding. I kept my faith.

Was death the start of my downfall?

Fear that if I let go, there would be nothing left?

In the end it would be death that would be the final termination of the person I had become.

The ice maiden has now been melted! And by letting go of the pain, keeping my faith has brought love and joy back into my heart, my world.

Is life an illusion?

They say everything comes out in the wash. I had been thrown in the high tech washing machine of life, proceeded onto and dragged along the conveyor belt of change. Then I headed straight for the life wringer, to squeeze out every last bit of shit that was stored up inside. The stored up shit I had collected. It had to go, the childhood shit, adult shit, broken hearts, losing loved one, families that have been broken apart. Everything always comes out in the wash.

Dealing with suppressed emotions, the betrayals and death. I now feel liberated, true to myself. I feel shit free! Do I need a religion? There are a few religions that I definitely would not choose. The nonsense and bullshit of the Catholic Church with all its bent priests, who faced convictions, trials and ongoing investigations into allegations of sex crimes committed by the priests and members of religious orders. Christianity wants people to conform to the many rules to keep them in check. Christianity produces sexually misery and youths are left feeling guilt ridden with regards to any sexual desires, even masturbation is classed as a sin. How can touching your own body be a sin? The murders and persecution of Pagans, the witch hunts.. Christians burnt alive anyone claiming to be the son of God, not noticing the irony that this was how Jesus was treated. Witch hunting was Christianity's worst crime – men woman and small children were tortured to death. The Cross – many people assume that the cross is a Christian symbol. Christians have indeed adopted the cross but its origin dates back long before the Messiah was ever born. The cross can be dated back to ancient Babylon and the worship of the sun – gods Mithra and Tammuz. In fact the cross was not used by Christians until the fourth century after Emperor Constantine (a pagan sun-worshipper) had a vision of the cross in front of the sun.

Muslims, who consider the division of God's oneness to be a grave sin and also kill women for her loving somebody her family disapproves of, by stoning her to her death, they rape women before her execution, this is supposed to bring the interrogator a spiritual reward equivalent to making the mandated Haj pilgrimage. No God would give any spiritual reward to such sickening acts against woman. The Islam faith allows men to marry young girls, many girls as young as nine A man can marry a girl younger than nine years of age, even if the girl is still a baby. A man, however is prohibited from having intercourse with a girl younger than nine, other sexual act such as foreplay, rubbing, kissing and sodomy is allowed. Islam began killing non believer's right from the start, slaughter (Jihad) and oppression (sharia) killing for Islam is not a modern idea. This is not free will. Nor love. A woman should have the right to choose who she loves and who she chooses to make love to and not be punished. No man in the world regardless of his religion should be allowed to have sex or perform any form of sexual act on a child.

So where did religion start? Every religion has its own view. Some say it all started in Persia and that this religion encourages humans to follow three things if they want to be prosperous in their life;

1.good thought 2.good speech 3.good deed.

There are no other rules in it. Every human should search and see what is good for them, what works. What makes them happy, what makes them feel good about themselves and start doing it and try to make the world a better place. Religion has brought nothing but hatred and competition between all cultures and societies, including wars and terrorism. When was the last time you heard of an Atheist terrorist or a Theist fundamentalist. But this is only my belief and with free will. We each can decide for ourselves what our own path is, our own faith. We can all choose what we want to believe in what feels right in our hearts. It is a man own mind that causes evil. It is all about love the rest is made up bullshit.

Did I save my soul? Save my life and restore my beliefs? Or did I take all my fears out of the cardboard box in my head and put them in the shed? The shed! Put them in a shed...I locked them in a cell.

Soul retrieval is that what this game has been all about. This mad roller coaster of the real life ghost train speeding in my own private carriage three thousand miles per hour and why? Was I inpatient? Did I meddle in magic?

I had transformed into somebody I did not recognize anymore, someone I never set out to be. I wanted true love, true love romance. I wanted the ultimate fairy cake with all five ingredients. The icing on the cake and a cherry for me!

Death – When I saw my soul standing on the ledge, my vision. Could it be that I was too scared to jump – to let go? Was I thinking I hope this harness keeps me safe in here, I am going down baby, I bought the ticket I am getting on ....Hold on tight...Choo choo!

Other visions I had warning me before hand that that this was going to be a tough road, the little people trying to push the rock up the hill?

Are my visions real?

Or

Am I mad?

Psychosis, magic, sixth sense!

Did I click my fingers and change my world? Could it be that after the demands to my God to change my world, fear set in?

Or did I demand too much to change all at once?

Be not afraid of growing be only afraid of standing still...

Did I ride the train that was to roller coaster me into another life, into another place? Did I go through the ultimate test of faith?

Did that or did that not just happen?

Plodding along in life then I do a u turn, go down three thousand miles down to the very pit at the bottom of the shit.

Living with the dead who sucked the soul out of me, Was I in the pit? Or was my soul already in the pit I had to go down to get it back? Lost in the darkness caring the burden of all the weight from the shit.

So the train journey of my life that what was. No longer is.

Do I have faith? Do I believe? Is there something more, something bigger out there? in the big galaxy that surrounds our tiny little bullshit worlds. Where we are caught up in shit living and realizing we do not even know ourselves. Do we sell our self short everyday living in a life that does not make us truly happy, truly fulfilled, truly satisfied?

Something was missing from me and that something was my soul, something that material flakiness and bullshit could not satisfy. I was searching for my heart's desire, my passions, me. I knew deep down I really wanted this change.

I knew deep inside what I wanted to be, to be free. I could feel it deep down inside of me. I knew I was on the wrong path. I knew that somewhere, something definitely went wrong but I did not know how to change it. What happened? And how did I get here?

I say this with incredible gratefulness appreciation and gratitude and also because I am curios. I asked questions and questions and still more questions. I wanted back my connection, my inner peace, my true form, I wanted back what gives me comfort and joy.

As I was driving down the street one day, dropping out of the sky was a bird, at first I thought it was a rock but I swear to God, as he is my witness I saw this bird smash into my car window screen, it was real, it was a bird, no shit, I still ask myself the very same question today. Did that happen? This bird came crashing down onto my car window screen at a million miles per hour and then bounced off like a tennis ball, just like that, as it was hurtling forward in to my direction all I could do was stare 'what the fuck is that -I didn't know what to do, slam on my breaks or speed up, I instead just took my foot of the accelerator and hopped for the best - did that just happen?' a rock would have landed on my car window screen and wiped me out. I was freaked out and a little panicky, birds just don't fall out of the sky! What the fuck?! Am I seeing things?

I am mad!

I asked for signs, they came in quick and in the most really strange bizarre ways and I say thank you for everything that has happened because I had asked for it.

Did that just happened?

Change- is one of the hardest lessons in life. It could be love, loss, anger or guilt, change is never easy you fight to hold on then you fight to let go.

I screamed for change in a cell. I prayed and meditated in a cell. I then faced my fears in a cell, on my own in the silence, my journey of three.

Did I ride the train? Did I sit on the seat? Is it real or is it just an illusion. This existence we call life? Are we spiritual beings having a human experience? Is Earth a test?

Am I using my power of thought, casting spells, saying my prayers to change my world?

Am I creating the reality I want to exist in?

Or

Am I mad?

FLORA – THE GODDESS OF SPRING

Flora "flourishing one" was the Roman Goddess of flowers, garden and spring. She was especially associated with vines, olives, all kind of fruit trees and honey bearing plants. Her temple was situated in the vicinity of Circus Maximus and her worship was said to be introduced by Numa. She is the embodiment of all nature; her name has come to represent all plant life. She is especially the Goddess of power, including the flower of youth. Her festivals of unrestraint pleasure, the floralia, was celebrated at the end of April and beginning of May. This festival was probably the origins of the maypole dance and the gathering of bouquets and flowers, symbolizing the beginning of spring and new life into the world. She gives charm to youths, aroma to wine, sweetness to honey and fragrance to blossoms.

Flora teaches us to honour growing things both inside and outside us. She is a reminder to pay attention to pleasure, to the beauty of spring and to new life wherever it is found.

Although the Ancient Roman holiday Floralia, celebrated by the set of games and theatrical presentations known as the Luni Florales, began in April, it was really an ancient May Day celebration. Flora, the Roman Goddess in whose honour the festival was held was the Goddess of flowers which generally began to bloom in spring. The holiday for flora as officially determined by Julius Caesar when he ran from April 28th to May 3rd.

The Lundi was financed by minor public magistrates know as audiles. The curule audiles was originally 365B.C. limited participants, but was later opened up to plebeians too. The Lundi could be very expensive for the audiles who used the games as a way of winning affection and votes of the people. In this way, the audiles hoped to ensure victory in future elections for higher office they had finished their year as audiles.

The Flora festivals began in Rome in 238 B.C to please the Goddess

Flora into protecting the blossoms. The Florlia fell out of favour and was discontinued until 173 B.C when they senate concerned with the wind, hail and other damaged to flowers ordered Flora's celebration reinstated as the Lundi Florales.

The Lundi florales included theatrical events including mimes, naked actresses and prostitutes. In the renaissance some writers thought that Flora had been a human prostitute who was turned into a goddess, possibly because of the licentiousness of Lundi Florales. Flora was a common name for prostitutes in ancient Rome.

The celebration in honour of Flora included floral wreaths worn in the hair.

Cross – many people assume that the cross is a Christian symbol. Christians have indeed adopted the cross but its origin dates back long before the Messiah was ever born. The cross can be dated back to ancient Babylon and the worship of the sun – gods Mithra and Tammuz. In fact the cross was not used by Christians until the fourth century after Emperor Constantine (a pagan sun-worshipper) had a vision of the cross in front of the sun.

Ankh – also known as the long life seal. While Christians try to say the Ankh is not a cross, make no mistake about it the ankh is indeed another rendering of cross. This symbol originated in Egypt and symbolizes reincarnation. Egyptians were pagans and worshiped many gods like the sun-god Amen-Rah, and the pagan sun-trinity: Osiris, Isis and Horus. The ankh and the common cross were both used equally in ancient pagan sun-worship.

Fish symbol – also known at the Ichthys symbol (Greek for fish). Another adaptation of a pagan symbol into Christianity the fish was used worldwide as religious symbol associated with the pagan "Great Mother Goddess" It was meant to represent the outline of her vulva. It is linked to the age Pisces and also has association with the Hindu deity Vishnu but more so Dagon the fish-god of the philistines. The name Dagon is derived from dag which means fish. There have also been discoveries of the fish-god in sculptures found in Nineveh Assyria. Dagon is also found in the Scriptures (Judges 16:23-24; Samuel 5:-5)

Triquetra Symbol – another symbol adopted by Christianity. This symbol is used to symbolize the Christian trinity doctrine, however this symbol was originally used to represent the Three- Part Goddess (Maiden, Mother, Crone).

Peace – Also known as the cross of Nero. Many people are not aware of the origins of this symbol or how it became to symbolize peace. This is the cross of Nero, a broken cross, enclosed in a circle which represented Nero's vision. Nero believed that there would be world peace without Christianity. Thousands of Christians were martyred under the rule of Nero. This is what the peace sign represents regardless of what it means to you.

Peace and Happiness.

CPSIA information can be obtained
at www.ICGtesting.com
Printed in the USA
BVHW031142291019
562359BV00001B/6/P